DATE DUE

TIME OF THE EAGLE

BOOKS DONATED BY LITERACY COUNCIL OF JEFFERSON COUNTY

Thanks to UGN,
the Port Townsend and the
East Jefferson County Rotaries,
and the Brinnon/Quilcene
Garden Club for supporting the
Literacy Council of Jefferson
County's Multicultural
Book Project.

TIME OF THE EAGLE

by

Stephanie Golightly Lowden

BLUE HORSE BOOKS

Blue Horse Books is an imprint of Midwest Traditions, Inc., of Milwaukee, Wisconsin, a nonprofit press working to create books of lasting quality for young readers. Our books are available from your favorite bookstore. For a complete catalog of all our titles or to place a special order, visit our website:

www.bluehorsebooks.org

Time of the Eagle, © 2004, Stephanie Golightly Lowden

This is a work of fiction. The characters are drawn from the imagination, and any resemblance to actual persons living or dead is coincidental.

Blue Horse Books first published this title as an original trade softcover in 2004; the hardcover edition followed in 2006.

ISBN-13: 978-1-883953-38-6 (hardcover ed.)
ISBN-10: 1-883953-38-3 (hardcover ed.)
ISBN-13: 978-1-883953-34-8 (softcover ed.)
ISBN-10: 1-883953-34-0 (softcover ed.)

Library of Congress Cataloging-in-Publication Data

Lowden, Stephanie Golightly, 1949-
    Time of the eagle / by Stephanie Golightly Lowden.
        p. cm.
    Summary: In 1781, thirteen-year-old Autumn Dawn and her six-year-old brother Coyote Boy flee the smallpox that is rampant in their home village and struggle to survive the winter as they search for their Ojibwa Indian relatives. Includes historical notes.
    Includes bibliographical references (p.).
    ISBN 1-883953-34-0 (pbk. : alk. paper)
    1. Ojibwa Indians – History – 18th century – Juvenile fiction. [1. Ojibwa Indians – History – 18th century – Fiction. 2. Smallpox – History – Fiction. 3. Survival – Fiction. 4. Brothers and sisters – Fiction.] I. Title.
PZ7.L9616Ti 2004
[Fic] – dc22
                                        2003068856

Cover design by Mighty Media, Minneapolis

Acknowledgements

I would like to thank all the people I've met and worked with over the years at the Wisconsin Historical Museum. If I had never become a docent, this book would never have been born.

Many thanks to the staff of the Wisconsin Historical Society library and archives for helping me locate the many resources I needed. Thanks also to Bob Birmingham for answering a number of my questions.

Thanks to Hap Gilliland at the Council for Indian Education who read this book first and encouraged me to find a publisher. Thanks also to the Ojibwe people I consulted who gave me much needed advice.

Many thanks to my editor, Philip Martin, for working so diligently to get it right.

Thanks to my writer's group: Sheri, Patty, Joan, Kathy, Karin, and Suzanne. Your encouragement and editing advice was, and is, invaluable.

Finally, thanks to Larry, Katie, and Jamie for putting up with my obsessions and always cheering me on. I cherish your belief in me.

I take responsibility for any and all errors that may appear in this novel. If I have misinterpreted some custom or way of speaking, it is my mistake and not the fault of any of the good people I've consulted.

Stephanie Golightly Lowden

For Terri,
who visits me only in dreams.
Sister, daughter, friend.
You are missed.

Chapter One

The fine, warm day of Wild Rice Moon clashed with the fear the young girl felt. In the forest, it was a time of special beauty, when the golden leaves of the aspen clamored for attention with the fiery orange of the maples. But Autumn Dawn saw none of it. This year, the dying out of summer meant the dying of her people.

She stepped closer to her mother. But the girl stopped as her mother drew back, almost stumbling, but trying to keep a distance between them.

"Mother, you are ill." Autumn Dawn was afraid to take another step. She couldn't shake the numbness growing inside her. Surely, none of this was happening.

"Do not come near," her mother cried out. Fear, and the fever, caused her mother's weak voice to waver as the woman stood, hunched over with pain, in front of the small birchbark-covered lodge.

"I will not leave you, Mother. Someone must care for you." Autumn Dawn argued, defying her mother for the first time in her thirteen years.

"You will go, Daughter," her mother answered, "and not only because I ask it of you." Mother glanced at the small boy holding Autumn Dawn's hand.

Autumn Dawn looked at Coyote Boy. Her little brother's eyes brimmed with tears. He might not understand all that was taking place, but he knew that his Mother was sending them away.

"But Mother, if I leave . . ." she hesitated. The smoke from the smoldering bearskin intensified the numbness growing inside her—the feeling that none of this could be real. The bearskin, now smoking on the fire, was ready to burst into flame. It had once hung across the doorway to her father's fever wigwam. When he'd grown ill, Father had insisted on living separately from them. Now he was gone. He had joined their ancestors, and Mother was burning the skin.

The smoke made Autumn Dawn feel like a thin veil existed between herself and the real world. If only she could break through that cloudy curtain, perhaps everything would again be the way it used to be—before the trader's illness came. Father, and her best friend, White Otter, she could almost see them. . . .

Autumn Dawn Shines on Leaf shook herself and tried to speak calmly. "But Mother, there are none left here—no one to care for you."

"If you two children stay, both of you will die, too."

"Perhaps not. We have heard stories that some have lived after having the fever. We are a strong people. I could care for you until you are well. And then . . ."

The girl tried to sound confident, but her voice was

shaky. "And then, if Coyote Boy and I become ill . . . you can care for us."

Surely, Autumn Dawn thought, I can do something to make everything all right again. She squeezed Coyote Boy's little hand, and fought back the tears that wanted to come.

"Enough!" Mother rarely raised her voice. She backed away from Autumn Dawn. "I cared for your father until he journeyed to the Spirit World." Her voice softened only slightly. "I have seen what this disease can do—even to one so strong as he." She hesitated. And when she spoke again, her voice cracked with grief. "I will not have my children die so."

It was true. What some called the "trader's illness" had wiped out almost everyone, young and old, in their wild-rice camp. This camp was a gathering of families who spent each fall together, to harvest the wild rice, before separating off into smaller lodges for the winter.

The new illness was a horrible disease. The first sign was a high fever, the same fever Autumn Dawn now saw in her mother's eyes. Next, the victim would break out in ugly red spots that oozed a hideous yellow liquid. After that—death.

Seeing her mother's pain tore apart the curtain of numbness that had surrounded Autumn Dawn. A sudden stab of sorrow pierced her like a hunter's spear. She lowered her eyes and looked away from the flushed face of her mother. "I will do as you wish, Mother." Her throat closed around the words.

"Mama?" Coyote Boy cried out as he tried to move toward his mother, but Autumn Dawn held on firmly.

"No!" Mother commanded. "You must go with Autumn Dawn now, my son. You will be safe with her. Go to my sister's family to the north. They will take care of you."

Autumn Dawn Shines on Leaf swept her little brother into her arms. Although he was only six years old, his small muscles were sturdy, strong. He tried desperately to get away. Autumn Dawn looked at her mother's feverish face one more time. There would be no hug of good-bye like other times when the girl had gone off to visit relatives. "Mother . . ."

"Go. Go now, children. Find our relatives. Save yourselves." Her mother turned her back on them and quickly disappeared into the fever lodge.

Autumn Dawn lifted the small boy onto her hip, turned, and ran. Coyote Boy wailed. She would run north, like Mother had said. Never mind the constant slamming into her side of the weight of her little brother's body. Never mind that his sorrowful cries rang in her ears. She too, would have liked to cry, but there was no time for weeping. Later, maybe, when they were safe with her mother's sister's family.

The forest breeze mingled the scent of freshly fallen leaves with pine, but Autumn Dawn did not notice. Only the scent of smoldering bearskin remained with her.

Although she avoided the downed trees and large rocks on the well-worn path leading away from the village to the north, she saw none of it.

Finally, she could run no longer. She must stop, to catch her breath. Deep in the woods, with the village now far behind, Autumn Dawn spotted a large round boulder in a clearing, with a flat spot on top. She set Coyote Boy down upon it.

"Little Brother," she said, her breath coming in short gasps, "you will have to walk on your own now. You must be a strong little warrior, even if you are only six summers old."

The small child looked up at her, tears streaking his round face. He stopped his wailing, though, and his eyes were trusting of his big sister. "I will be brave, Autumn," he said. He always called her that, Autumn Dawn Shines on Leaf being too long for his young tongue.

Autumn remembered the story of how she had been given her name. On the morning of her birth, the first thing her mother had seen when the lodge flap had been opened was the morning sun shining on a bright red leaf. "It was the happiest day of my life," Mother had said.

But today, the memory sent another piercing stab of sorrow through her heart. Like a drum, her heart beat hard after the long run from the village. She was exhausted.

She gathered her little brother in her arms, holding him close. As she sank down with him into the moist ferns of the forest floor, a terrible fear grew inside her. She slowly breathed in the cool, pine-scented air, but still she could not shake the fear.

What if she didn't find her relatives? Mother had given them directions and she knew the way well. They should arrive by nightfall. She had very few supplies with her: just a small amount of rice and tobacco in her medicine bag and of course, her knife, which no Anishinaabe would be without.

If only White Otter were here. Together, she had thought they could face anything. Tall and strong, her dearest friend White Otter had been the best of the young hunters. But when the illness came to their camp, not even his strength could defeat it.

She gasped out loud. How could she live with so much loss? Then she felt her brother's small, warm body against her own and knew the answer. *I must be strong now, for the safety of my little brother. I will not think of those who have gone to the other side.*

Autumn Dawn stood up. It was time to move on.

Just then, she thought she saw something out of the corner of her eye. Carefully, she scanned the woods for any sign of danger, but there was nothing.

The morning light streamed through the trees. Ahead, rising from a high point just off to the side of the trail, was a tall, dead pine. Her eyes stung with the glare as she looked up at it. Coyote Boy stood up and tugged on her leg.

An eagle perched on the very top of the dead tree. Suddenly the bird launched itself off the ancient branch. The sun glanced off its bright white head, as the huge wings flapped three times and then soared. She watched as he moved easily, dipping this way, then that, on the light wind. Over the treetop, he sped off and up into the sky, gliding on the breezes of Wild Rice Moon.

Eagle had come to her before, she recalled, when she had needed guidance—during a girlhood dream fast, when she had waited and listened for a helper to appear. Now he was back, climbing in a slow circle higher and higher. Then, he flew away in a straight line, with the slow beat of his long, powerful wings.

Autumn took a deep breath. "This is a good sign, Little Brother. I am sure of it." Eagle, she felt, was to be her protector.

The eagle, now a mere dot in the sky, was headed northwest; it was the way her relatives lived. Autumn Dawn took Coyote Boy's hand, and they resumed their journey.

As they walked in the direction the eagle had taken, Autumn was thankful the day was fair and cool. For this time of the year, it was almost warm. Her spirits rose, just a little.

Not long after that, they came upon a large lake. The breeze had disappeared and the air was still. In the blue water, the trees were reflected clearly as if in a trader's mirror. Pure, clean, life-giving *Nibi*.

Gichi-manidoo, Great Spirit, Autumn Dawn prayed, *watch over us so these lakes continue to give life to our people, rather than witness more death.*

The sun was high in the sky now and Coyote Boy was tired. She studied the area carefully. Was this the lake where she, her mother, and the other women of the summer camp had so often set their fishing nets? Yes, it was. She and her brother had traveled farther than she thought, for this was some distance from their wild-rice gathering camp which they'd left only that morning. Recognizing the lake gave her a feeling of great relief. Her aunt's house would be near.

"We will eat soon, Little Brother." She looked down at the small boy and squeezed his hand.

He looked at her, and his tiny smile was her mother's. For a moment she thought she would weep, but Autumn stopped herself. Focusing her thoughts, she looked around and spotted a chokecherry tree. It still bore fruit so she quickly picked some and handed them to Coyote Boy. She squinted, trying to see into the woods that surrounded her and the lake.

There was a small wigwam, not far from the lake on the shore off to her right. Perhaps it was her relatives' lodge. This was the place she remembered they often spent time during the Wild Rice Moon.

"Come along, Little Brother, our journey may be over."

Coyote Boy smiled at her, cherry juice dripping from his puckered mouth. Autumn Dawn took his hand and smiled. In many ways, he was still a baby.

As they neared the wigwam, Autumn grew more cautious. The shelter was awfully small, and was obviously put together in haste. Surely, this couldn't be her aunt's lodge. A hastily built hunter's shelter maybe?

"Stay here," she said to her brother.

Reluctantly the little boy let go of her hand and she walked slowly toward the lodge.

When she saw the door was missing, Autumn Dawn stopped. The picture of her mother burning the bearskin door of the fever wigwam that morning flashed into her mind. Perhaps her aunt had done the same? With heart beating fast, she resumed her approach to the small lodge.

Then she smelled it—the stench of illness and death. Someone had died inside this wigwam. But who?

Slowly, she took a few more steps. Her stomach felt queasy from the odor. Careful not to touch anything, Autumn stood in the entrance to the wigwam and cautiously peered in. On the floor was her aunt's body, insects already feasting on it. The hideous rash of the fever dotted the woman's skin.

Autumn Dawn screamed.

Chapter Two

"Autumn!" Coyote Boy cried out at her side.

"No! Do not come near! It is not safe here." Autumn Dawn Shines on Leaf grabbed his hand and for the second time that day ran away from the sickness that was killing her people.

"I am a fool," she muttered to herself as they ran back to the lake. She didn't want him to know how scared she was. She never should have screamed like that. Of course he would come looking for her. He could have run into the wigwam, caught the illness. She had promised her mother she'd protect him. That was her only task now. It must be her only thought.

They returned to the lakeshore. There was no trace of her cousins or uncle. Autumn scanned the horizon, looking . . . for what, she did not know. Where would they go now? What if they found no one before the killing winds of winter swept down from the north? The image of her dead aunt swam before her eyes. She fought back the tears and straightened her shoulders. There would be time to grieve later. Now she must make a plan.

Then, she saw him again: *migizi*, Brother Eagle. He flew in wide arcs over the lake, sweeping low as if searching for fish. He swept closer to the shore, dipping down, now almost skimming the water. For just an instant, he hovered over a spot on the lake only about twenty feet from where Autumn stood. Then in another moment, he was gone, sailing over the treetops, again heading northwest.

Something told Autumn to look more closely into the clear lakewater where the eagle had hovered. At first, she thought what she saw was a loon that had dived under the water for fish. But as she looked closer, she realized it could not be a loon. In fact, it was not a living thing at all. As her eyes focused better on the triangular object, she grew curious.

"Stay here," she commanded her little brother as she waded out into the lake.

The water was cold, and Autumn knew she would regret her curiosity once the sun went down. Still, something about the object seemed familiar. Then, as she drew closer she realized what it was: the prow of a canoe.

"A canoe!" she shouted to Coyote Boy. As was the way of the Anishinaabe, someone had sunk a canoe underwater for the winter. Only the end of it was visible, sticking up out of the lake. Birchbark canoes needed water as much as the People needed canoes. Late in the fall, they were sunk in lakes so they would stay moist during the winter months when not in use.

Autumn, soaked now to the top of her buckskin dress, pulled the heavy rocks out of the canoe bottom, then dragged it to shore. Coyote Boy danced with joy as she pulled it in.

"We have a way to travel, Little Brother. Surely, we'll find our people quickly now."

"Whose is it?" Coyote Boy said.

"Probably it belonged to our aunt and uncle." They would have no use for it now. "But I think finding it is a gift from Eagle."

She tipped the canoe over to get the remaining water out and then set it in the sun. They would stay here for a few hours until the canoe was dried out enough to use. Meanwhile, she would look for food and any medicinal plants they might need on their journey. She hoped the sun would dry her dress out while she searched.

Later, when Coyote Boy was well stuffed with cherries, and her medicine bag filled with a fresh supply of healing roots, they set off in the now dry canoe. At first, paddling the clear lake, Autumn felt exhilarated. This was her home, these lakes and woods. She would choose to live nowhere else. The sun glinting off the lake mesmerized her in a way only water and light could. It reminded her of the day she stood on the lakeshore with White Otter. The sunset had been like a golden waterfall of light, broken only by the tree line.

Autumn Dawn blinked back tears and cleared her mind. The time for daydreaming was past. Later, when

Coyote Boy was safe, perhaps there would be time for new dreams.

As the sun disappeared, a blanket of cold air settled over the canoe. Coyote Boy was shivering and Autumn Dawn thought it best to make camp. Her little brother helped her push the canoe on shore, getting as soaked as she had been earlier.

"Quickly, Brother, collect some dried-out birchbark for tinder. We must get a fire going or you will freeze to death in those wet clothes." She ignored her own discomfort in the buckskin dress that was still slightly damp from the lake waters.

It took awhile to get a fire started, as Autumn did not have any piece of trader's steel with her. So she searched the shore for two good stones that, when struck hard together, would create a bright spark. Then she shredded the birchbark that Coyote Boy had collected into a small, loose pile.

For what seemed like an eternity, Autumn patiently huddled over the little pile and struck one stone against the other, time after time, until a spark dropped and caught like a small firefly in the shredded birchbark.

Quickly, she bent close and blew carefully on it, and was delighted, and relieved, to see the brief spark grow to a tiny flame. Soon, the fire was roaring. Autumn Dawn felt some comfort; she had managed to provide food and warmth for her brother. All they needed now was shelter.

"Little Brother, would you like to help me make a lodge for us?"

"Oh yes," Coyote Boy answered enthusiastically. He loved to help with chores. Autumn knew he was anxious to feel grown up. Her fear was that he may have to grow up too soon on this journey.

There wasn't time to build a proper wigwam, but a simple shelter of branches would be sufficient for one night. Tomorrow they would continue their search for more Anishinaabe.

Quickly, with the skills her mother had taught her, Autumn Dawn began putting up a shelter made from young saplings and branches torn from downed pines. She built it near the fire, so they could keep warm while they slept. It would do for now. But if the winter storms came before they found the People, they would need a sturdier lodge. Autumn shut those thoughts out as she worked.

During the night Autumn Dawn woke up shivering. The wind was howling and she could feel a cold rain seeping through her hastily built shelter. Lacking bear-skins, she pulled Coyote Boy's small body close to her own and drifted back into a fitful sleep.

Sometime later she woke up to a tinkling sound, almost like the gourd shakers used with chanting to try to cure those sick with the trader's disease. But softer. As she became more aware of the source of the noise, though, she realized she was not back in her family's lodge. And it was not the sound of rattling shakers.

The rain was freezing. Winter had come.

When first light came, Autumn Dawn got up quietly so as not to disturb Coyote Boy. As she ventured out of their shelter, the cold air hit her like a slap. The trees were etched in white frost and the river was shrouded in an icy fog.

They would have to move quickly through the lakes and streams before the water froze over. On foot, traveling would be very difficult. Especially for the little one.

"Coyote Boy, wake up. We must set out early today."

The child moaned in his sleep and turned over.

Autumn Dawn shook him gently. "Little Brother, we must make haste." She put her hands under his arms and made him sit up. "Come," she said.

Coyote Boy blinked at her, "Mama?"

Autumn Dawn felt a pain where she knew her heart to be. "It's me, your sister."

Recognition and remembrance flashed in the little boy's eyes. Autumn fought back tears and picked the child up.

They had not traveled long when Coyote Boy began to complain of hunger.

"We will find some berries later. For now, Brother, we must travel as far as we can."

But Coyote Boy kept up his complaint, and Autumn Dawn found herself growing impatient with him. She stopped paddling for a moment, arms stiff and sore, and scolded, "We have to keep going, don't you see? We will die out here all alone. We have to find someone, some distant relative or friend to live with through the winter. We cannot stop to eat. Now, hush."

She resumed her paddling.

But Coyote Boy did not hush. Instead, he began to cry. Autumn Dawn put up with it for a while, but finally she grew exasperated. "Stop it, now. No more crying, do you hear me?" she shouted.

Coyote Boy did stop then, but his silence was almost worse. His solemn eyes made her angry. Didn't he know she was doing everything she could to help them find other Anishinaabe? Why did he stare at her with that trusting face? Didn't he know she was lost?

There, she admitted it. She was lost. Yes, she knew how to get back to her mother's camp, but what good would that do? Everyone there was dead by now. But to continue northwest—she didn't know this country. She knew that to the west somewhere lived their enemies, the ones that her people called the *Bwaan*. The Bwaan were quarreling with her people over territory. Sometimes they fought, when a group of her people encountered a party of the Bwaan.

Her father had once explained to her that as the light-skinned traders came in greater numbers, other tribes were pushing at the Anishinaabe from the east. And the Anishinaabe were pushing in turn into the hunting lands of the Bwaan.

It seemed to a young child that there was enough land for all to live together peacefully, and Autumn Dawn had said so to her father. Maybe you are right, he said, but he did not sound like he believed it. He had told her stories meant to scare her, to keep from wandering off alone into the woods.

Now, what if they met a group of Bwaan? Would they agree with her that there was enough hunting land for all, and let her and her brother go in peace? Or would they take the two children as prisoners and carry them off, far away from her people? Or might they be killed?

"Stop it!" she cried out loud, desperate to defeat her panic. Coyote Boy burst into tears.

Autumn Dawn stopped paddling. She had frightened the poor child. He thought she was yelling at him. "There, there, Little One." She leaned over and patted his hand. "I am sorry. I wasn't talking to you. I was just . . . talking."

He looked up at her, so vulnerable and small. The child was too small for such a journey. He needed food, meat preferably, to stay strong. She would have to slow down and find him some.

"We will rest, now. I will make a rabbit snare." She sat up straight and looked at him. "Do you think you can catch a partridge?" Sometimes even small children could catch the slow, strutting birds by simply coming up behind them and dropping a noose over their heads.

Coyote Boy's eyes lit up. Autumn Dawn could feel her own mouth watering at the prospect of real food. She picked up her paddle and headed toward shore with short but confidant strokes.

It took a while to make Coyote Boy's snare. Mother would have used twine made from the basswood tree. Autumn Dawn did not have time for that process. Instead, she used long strips of peeled roots, cut with her knife from trees growing right along the shoreline.

By the time she was done, she too was starving. Coyote Boy took the partridge snare and quietly walked a little ways off into the woods.

Autumn went about fashioning the rabbit snare, a net made from the peeled tree-roots. When she was done, she walked out into the forest and found what looked like a promising spot. First, she took a pinch of tobacco out of her medicine bag. Sprinkling it over the earth, she made an offering to the Great Spirit.

Then, with the snare set, she went about the task of building a sturdier shelter than the one they had slept in the night before. It wasn't much more than a lean-to, but this time she made sure the biggest cracks were covered by pine boughs to keep the cold out.

She must protect Coyote Boy from snows which could come even this early in the season. She wondered about her decision to follow the eagle north. Perhaps she should head south, where the winters were warmer? But her people had always lived in the north.

As for the eagle, he hadn't shown himself lately.

Why was she so confused? If only she were traveling alone. She could accept any fate for herself, but not for her little brother. She must make the right decision. She must be strong.

When she was finished building the shelter she looked to the sky, hopefully, searching for Eagle. But the skies were empty. *What should I do?* she wanted to scream, but didn't. She would not frighten Coyote Boy again.

"Autumn, I found some berries," Coyote Boy's voice interrupted her thoughts. Autumn Dawn turned around to see her little brother with a handful of wilted red berries. The bird snare dangled in his other hand.

"Let me see, Little One." She took the berries and inspected them. As she had feared, the frost last night had been a killing one. The berries were shriveled and soft to the touch.

"You may try one." She smiled at him. The frost would have changed the berries, so she wasn't sure Coyote Boy would like them.

Coyote Boy took a bite. "Ptooey!" He spat it out. "It is too soft."

"You should still try to eat some. But don't worry, our snares will be full soon enough."

She hoped it was true.

Chapter Three

Later, when Autumn Dawn Shines on Leaf went out with the bird snare, she was able to tiptoe up behind and catch a partridge—a single, tiny bird. She had brought along some tinder from their last camp, so this time, the starting of a fire was quicker. Soon it was crackling away inside their shelter, and a meager dinner of bird meat and a handful of wild rice was ready. She gave all the meat to Coyote Boy, without him knowing. He ate it eagerly and then fell asleep.

Autumn Dawn ate only some of the rice. She would have to find more food soon, if they were to have the strength to continue their journey.

After checking on Coyote Boy one last time, to be sure he was truly asleep, she ventured out into the woods. It was twilight. During the day the frost had melted, but the cloudless sky told Autumn the night would be cold once again.

The lake and woods had taken on a golden glow where the sun shone on the eastern shore. She quickly went about her work, resetting the rabbit snare. Her stomach ached with hunger and fear. If only she could kill a deer.

Women in her family were not trained in the skill of hunting. Autumn Dawn didn't have a bow or any arrows with her. But as she finished her tasks and returned to the fire, the idea nagged at her. She, kill a deer? The more she thought about it, the more she knew it was the only way they'd survive the winter. Surely, she could make her own bow and some arrows. She'd seen her father do it many times. Just recently he had showed Coyote Boy how. Maybe her little brother could help.

Autumn Dawn stared into the fire, her mind spinning. Making a bow and arrows would be child's play compared to the actual hunt. Her father sometimes would track a deer several days before successfully bringing it down. Could she do that? She would have Coyote Boy with her; that would complicate things.

Or would it? Father had already taken her brother on two or three hunting trips. Perhaps her little brother knew more than she realized. They would discuss it in the morning.

Shivering, Autumn Dawn moved closer to the small fire. There was no choice. They not only needed the deer meat to eat, but they needed its hide to make warm winter clothing. They would freeze to death without it. She reached for Coyote Boy and gently moved him next to her. Autumn laid down, her little brother curled in her arms, and went to sleep thinking of the deer.

She awoke with first light, a cold wind whipping over her face and body. Coyote Boy, almost smothered by her protective embrace, seemed warm enough. She thought she must have given him all her warmth because she felt as if she would crack like an icicle when she stood up.

"Coyote Boy," she whispered, "it is time to wake up." The little boy moaned and moved in her arms.

"Come now, sleepy one. I need your help today."

Coyote Boy opened his eyes. "Do you have a job for me, Sister?"

"Yes," she answered as she helped him sit up. "We are going to hunt a deer."

Coyote Boy's eyes went wide. "A deer?" he exclaimed.

"Yes, a deer," she said firmly, feeling far less sure of herself than she sounded.

Coyote Boy scrambled to his feet. "I can hunt the deer, Autumn. You can stay here and trap the little animals." He put his hands on his hips and puffed out his chest.

Autumn laughed. "I think I had better do the actual killing, Brother. You are still a little too small." Coyote Boy frowned.

She stood up too and put wood on the fire. "Come. You can help me make the bow and arrows. We will put father's special mark on them." She remembered how her father would toil over his arrows until they came out just right. The memory sent a spear of grief straight through her heart again.

"I will look for just the right wood. I know what father used." His disappointment forgotten, Coyote Boy danced around their fire in glee.

His eagerness soothed Autumn's grief. "First, we will check our snare and see to a meal. Then, we will look for wood."

This time, her net snare held a decent-sized rabbit. At least they would have a little to eat, and the rabbit fur would make a warm lining for moccasins later—moccasins to be made from the skin of a deer. Autumn Dawn reset the snare, and they headed back to their shelter.

While the rabbit was left to roast over the fire, she and Coyote Boy began to look for just the right branches to fashion a bow and arrows. "Perhaps tomorrow our snare will be full again," Autumn Dawn said to him as she kept a watchful eye on the roasting meat nearby.

Her little brother seemed to forget his hunger once he started searching the woods. Autumn was glad he was such a strong little worker. It didn't take long to find just the right tree branches—from a hickory. She looked around for the nuts, but the squirrels had already taken them all.

Soon they were whittling wood into weapons. She and Coyote Boy took turns with the knife. His stubby little fingers were not coordinated enough to carve perfectly, but Autumn let him do a little of the work because it pleased him so. While they worked, Coyote Boy told her all he had learned from Father about bringing down the deer.

Autumn Dawn ate hungrily with her brother this time, her teeth tearing into the roasted rabbit meat. It would be her last meal for awhile. Tomorrow, she would fast.

For tomorrow, she would hunt the deer.

Chapter Four

It was much later that night when Autumn Dawn Shines on Leaf and Coyote Boy finished making a bow and several arrows. First finding the right stones, and then chipping them into sharp points for arrowheads, had taken great patience. More than once, she had to start over when she had ruined a promising start with one wrong blow.

Coyote Boy helped for awhile, but she eventually had sent him off in the last light of day to try his luck with the bird snare. Soon, as the sky was darkening, he came back with a victorious smile and a small partridge. She cooked it and gave all the small amount of meat to her brother, along with the rest of the rice. He ate eagerly and soon fell asleep.

Autumn fed the fire and laid down beside the small boy. She knew they could not easily survive through the winter on the meat of a few small animals now and then.

She tried to concentrate on the deer she would search for tomorrow. It was customary to fast before, and sometimes during, the hunt. So, she would not eat tomorrow. Already her stomach ached just thinking about it. She hadn't eaten since the rabbit that morning and she was hungry now. Coyote Boy was young though, and he would need all his strength to search for the deer. In the morning she would check the net snare once more before setting out.

Autumn Dawn closed her eyes and tried to picture the deer, but no image came to her. She imagined herself walking into the thickest part of the forest. "Where are you?" her mind cried out. But there was no answer. Soon, she drifted off to sleep.

Autumn dreamed. The forest was cold and silent, without any animal sounds. No bird sang, no coyote howled. She walked on, and snow began to fall. Still, there were no deer tracks. Autumn Dawn shivered as she searched the woods, desperate to find any other living thing.

Suddenly, panic gripped her as she realized Coyote Boy was gone. She began to run, calling out her little brother's name. "Coyote Boy, where are you?" The icy wind swept over her, battering her exposed flesh. She began to sob. The tears froze on her cheeks as soon as they fell, turning her face into a stiff, hard mask.

"Coyote Boy," she called out, stumbling on something in the snow which grew ever deeper. She fell, the cold white snow encircling her body. Certain she was about to die, she pushed herself up onto her knees, curious what had tripped her.

At first, her eyes, almost frozen from the tears and cold, couldn't focus on the object that lay in the snow. She blinked back the last of her tears and squinted into the blinding white of the drift she'd fallen into. There, curled up with knees almost touching his chin, lay Coyote Boy.

Autumn Dawn leaned over to touch him. His naked body, a blue-gray color, did not stir.

"Coyote Boy?" she cried desperately, hoping he was still all right.

But his stiff corpse did not respond. Autumn tried to scream, but instead her face merely froze, her mouth gaping open.

She woke up, inside their tiny shelter, a strangled scream in her throat. Was this dream a foretelling? Would they both freeze to death on the hunt? Autumn's heart raced in her chest and she suddenly felt very small and unsure. She had never been on a hunt, and Coyote Boy was so young. He had seen six summers, but not yet six winters. What was she thinking of? Surely, she was not strong enough to do this thing.

Coyote Boy moaned in his sleep, as if he knew what she had been dreaming. Autumn pulled him close to her and edged them both towards the fire. Still, she shivered, more from fear than cold. Were they doomed to die out here, lost and alone? Or would they be captured by Bwaan warriors?

What about the eagle? Had he forgotten them?

Perhaps the Great Spirit had forgotten them as well. They were so small, and the endless woods so large.

No, she must not think that way. She would fast and pray harder so that the dream would not come true. She was thirteen, nearly an adult. She must do all she could to keep her little brother safe. There really was no choice but to hunt the deer. No choice at all. Autumn Dawn closed her eyes and went back to sleep.

When she awoke in the morning, Autumn tried to shake off the memory of the dream. "Little Brother, wake up. We must check the snare." The image of Coyote Boy, frozen in the snow, swam in front of her as she shook her brother gently. The small boy blinked sleep away and looked up at her.

"Today we hunt the deer," he said, his face proud and glowing with enthusiasm.

"Yes, Little One, we will begin the hunt today." She wished she could share his confidence. "But first you must eat something."

"But, Sister, Father always fasts before he hunts." He frowned at her.

"That may be, but you are too little to go without food."

"But, Autumn . . ." he began to whine.

Autumn looked at him, determined to win this battle. "You will eat." She said it with such finality she knew he would not argue. Just like Mother would have said it.

The thought made her wince with an inward pain.

Coyote Boy scowled at her, but said no more.

The dream-image of her little brother haunted her as they set off to check the snare. She tried to rid herself of it, but the stubborn picture refused to fade.

The snare held one small rabbit. Autumn Dawn quickly set about to roast it.

"I am finished, Sister," Coyote Boy said later, as he licked his lips and set most of the meat next to him on the floor of their small lodge.

Autumn frowned at him and glanced at the uneaten portion. "No, you are not."

"Yes, truly, Sister, I am no longer hungry. If I eat any more, I will surely burst."

"Burst? From such a small piece of meat?" She couldn't help but laugh at her determined brother.

"We can dry the rest of it, and I will take it with me on the hunt," he answered.

Autumn Dawn decided not to argue. The meat would keep. Coyote Boy would change his mind later, once his stomach started growling again.

Autumn re-set the snare before they left in case they returned that night—if they saw no sign of deer.

If they did find tracks, they wouldn't be returning. As hunters, they would follow the tracks, camping in the woods, possibly for several nights. It would be difficult to keep Coyote Boy warm and fed.

At least today, the air was a little warmer. If it stayed so mild, her brother would be all right.

But if it didn't snow, there would be no easy tracks to follow. It would be harder to find deer without snow.

They had been walking for some time. The dream-image of Coyote Boy returned to her often, but she brushed it away with a silent prayer. She kept a close watch on her little brother. So intent was he on finding tracks, he didn't notice her staring at him.

"Have you seen any sign of the deer yet, Brother?" she asked him.

"No, Sister, I have not. The deer is hiding from us today."

"Why don't we stop and rest for awhile? You can eat some of the leftover meat." Autumn stopped walking.

"Oh, no, Father would not do that. We must keep searching."

"Remember, Coyote Boy, I expect you to eat."

Coyote Boy stood still. He looked up at her with a questioning look. "Do you not remember last winter, Sister, when the owl followed Father and he said it was a bad sign? Both you and I fasted then, for good luck. And Father brought home a deer."

It was true. Her people believed Owl was bad luck for hunting. But they also believed that if the hunter's children fasted while the father was away, the bad luck could be turned to good. And indeed it had turned out that way last winter.

She looked hard at little Coyote Boy. Suddenly he seemed much older than his six years. "All right, Brother. If it is your wish, you may fast. But if you become too weak to travel, you will have to eat."

He grinned at her, smiling like a small child again. "Do not worry, Autumn, I can fast as well as you can. I will not become weak."

But as the day wore on, Autumn Dawn wasn't so sure of that.

Although they walked in a wide circle, studying the ground carefully, they did not cross any deer tracks. When the sun began to disappear behind the tall pines, Autumn led her brother back to the shelter.

They checked the net snare and found nothing, so Autumn sent Coyote Boy once more to try and capture a partridge. When he returned with two, her mouth began to water just looking at them. Coyote Boy's face told her he was as hungry as she.

"Will you eat now, Little One?" she asked him. She would continue to fast, but he should not.

"Maybe just a little, Autumn," he said in a tiny voice, as he took the partridges off their snares.

Autumn Dawn was so hungry that she left the shelter while the meat roasted, so as not to be tempted by it. She must continue her fast, not only for a successful hunt but also to keep last night's dream of losing Coyote Boy from coming true. She could only hope that it was a warning to her that she must try harder to do everything right.

The sky was free of clouds tonight. Stars shone brilliantly across the heavens. Autumn knew that on nights like this, when the white path of stars could be seen so clearly, it meant the next day would be cold.

They must find a deer soon. They would need the hide to keep warm.

"I am finished eating, Autumn." Coyote Boy's voice startled her as he came up behind her. She hadn't realized she'd been sitting there so long. "Will you sing a song to me, Autumn?"

Autumn Dawn was a good singer. One of the best in camp, her father had often told her. But the idea of singing reminded her too much of happy times in the past.

"No, Coyote Boy, I will not sing. After we kill a deer, then I will sing. Instead, I will tell you the story of Trickster and the helpful turtle. Sit down."

"Ooooh, I like that story," he answered with enthusiasm and sat down next to her.

"In the long ago time," she began, "*Wenabozho* was chasing Turtle because Turtle had been eating all the Anishinaabe People. Wenabozho wanted Turtle to stop eating his friends and do something useful instead. So one day he chased him with his bow and arrow.

"Turtle was swimming in the lake when he saw Wenabozho coming toward him. 'I am surely in trouble now,' he said to himself. Just as Wenabozho's arrow flew through the air toward Turtle, Turtle dove into the lake. When he did, his tail sent up a spray of water droplets.

"Wenabozho looked at the water droplets and laughed as he put away his bow and arrows. 'You have done something useful after all, Turtle,' he said as he changed the droplets into stars. 'The People will use these stars to help them find their way in all their comings and goings. This great path of light will also tell the birds when to fly south for the winter and when to return to the north country.'

"And that is why, Little Brother, Wenabozho was more than a Trickster. He helped our People in many ways."

Coyote Boy was leaning heavily against her arm now. Sleep had overtaken him. Autumn Dawn left Turtle's stars behind and carried her little brother back into the shelter.

One partridge remained on the spit. Her brother was a stubborn little boy. She shook her head as she laid him down on the mat. Ah well, at least he had eaten one of the birds.

Sleep came quickly that night for Autumn, exhausted from the day's hunt and the lack of food. No dreams disturbed her.

She awoke, surprised to see Coyote Boy and the sun already up. "How long have you been awake, Brother?" she asked as she rubbed the sleep from her eyes.

"Just a little while. I was about to wake you," he said as he put the last of their meat in his bag.

"Have you eaten?" she asked, already knowing the answer.

"Perhaps later, when I get hungry on the trail."

Autumn said no more as they left. Today, she led them farther from camp, following a series of narrow, well-worn deer paths along the nearby river that wandered from one thicket of brush to the next. But as the day wore on, and clouds took over the sky, Autumn Dawn began to wonder if maybe the deer were in hiding, perhaps in a cave somewhere, watching her and laughing.

They stopped for a rest and Coyote Boy ate some of the partridge meat. When he was finished, a light snow began to fall.

The large, slowly falling flakes chilled Autumn Dawn where her dress left her skin exposed. Her hunger, however, had disappeared. In its place, there was a dull ache inside her and a weakness to her step. Her eyes seemed to play tricks on her as well, as falling snow and brown autumn leaves seemed to blend in a foggy haze.

"Autumn, look!" Coyote Boy's voice jolted her awake. She'd been falling asleep as she walked.

Coyote Boy was pointing to the ground. "Look, Autumn, deer tracks."

"They must be fresh, Little Brother. It hasn't been snowing that long." The deer had to be close by.

Coyote Boy looked at her, puzzled. "Sister, it has been snowing all day."

Autumn looked to the west. The sun, a hazy globe,

was just above the horizon. Where had the day gone? Why did she feel as if they'd just set out? Never mind, they had found signs of the deer and must continue.

"We will follow the tracks until the sun is gone, Little One."

Soon it was almost too dark to see the tracks anymore, and Autumn Dawn had to admit that they had to stop for the night. They would make camp right here, so as not to lose the trail. Luckily, the snow had stopped. That meant the trail would still be visible the next day.

Coyote Boy was in a cheerful mood as they made a fire. "Tomorrow we will find the deer, Sister. I will bring it down with my bow and arrow!"

She smiled at him. She was pleased to see him so happy. "Eat some of the meat, Little One." It was the last of their food, and Autumn Dawn worried that they might not find more. The deer could elude them for days. They couldn't go back to their lodge by the river until they found him. Would Coyote Boy starve? Would she starve? She felt so weak this evening that she wondered if she would even awaken in the morning.

Autumn Dawn lay down next to the fire and watched her brother finish the meat.

"Do not worry, Sister. Tomorrow we will have deer meat."

An owl hooted nearby. Autumn Dawn Shines on Leaf shivered, hoping it wasn't a sign of bad luck to come.

Chapter Five

The next morning was warm, and although the warmth made the day pleasant, tracking the deer became far more difficult. Soon the trail turned to mud, and Autumn Dawn's moccasins made a squishing sound with each footfall. She could barely make out yesterday's deer tracks in the melting snow.

Today, the dull ache in her stomach had turned to pain. She glanced at Coyote Boy often, wondering if he were as hungry as she.

In late afternoon the trail finally led them to the edge of a raging river which fed into the river they had been following. The deer had crossed here. Autumn looked at her brother and back at the rushing waters. Even if they could cross it, they would both be soaked and risked freezing to death if they could not dry out before night fell.

A hopelessness began building in the pit of her stomach. It was too far to walk all the way back to their lodge to fetch their canoe. They would have to camp here for the night.

"We could cross it, couldn't we, Autumn?" Coyote Boy asked. His eyes looked hopeful, but Autumn saw something else there as well.

Hunger. Exhaustion. They could not continue.

"No, Brother. The waters are too rough and we would get too wet. If the night brings cold winds from the north, we could freeze to death. We have no other coverings." She gestured to her clothing.

Autumn stood for a while, watching the white water curling over itself as the river rushed by. She thought of the canoe they had left behind. By the time they went back to get it, the deer tracks would be cold. If only she were as strong and sure-footed as the deer.

Then, she heard a small sniffling noise. At first, she didn't know what it was. But then, she looked to her brother and saw that he was crying. It was the first time he had wept since the day they left Mother. She leaned over to pick him up, only to realize that she no longer had the strength. Instead she knelt down next to him.

"What troubles you, Little One?" she asked.

"It is all my fault, Autumn."

"What? What is all your fault?" she asked.

"We lost the deer because I did not fast. I should not have eaten the meat, Autumn. It was bad luck." He began sobbing pitifully then.

Autumn Dawn hugged her brother. "It is not your fault, Coyote Boy. The deer simply did not want to die today. Maybe tomorrow he will feel differently."

Coyote Boy's sobbing subsided, but Autumn wondered if her words were true. There was no easy way to cross the river. The deer would have to come to them. Or they would have to find a different deer. Autumn Dawn made a decision. Unless they saw new signs of the deer, they would return to the lodge in the morning so she could feed Coyote Boy. Then, they would set out again, on a new hunt, in a different direction.

She wondered how many days she could fast. She had felt a lightness about her head all that day, and her eyes had seen things that she was sure were not there. Perhaps she should give up her fast as well. But she would not think about it anymore tonight. She would not think about anything.

"Brother, let's make a fire and get some sleep. There is no more hunting to be done today."

Soon the fire was blazing. She lay down next to it, pulled her brother to her, and fell into a deep sleep.

In her dreams she again searched for Coyote Boy. "Little Brother, where are you?" she cried. But Coyote Boy gave no answer.

As before, there were no animal sounds in the woods. But this time there was no snow either. Instead, the forest was dark, almost black with patches of shadowy trees and limbs blocking her path. Smells of decaying plants sickened her. Then, she came upon a river, and she saw tracks.

But they were not the tracks of a deer. They were Coyote Boy's tracks.

She looked up quickly at the rushing river, the white

of its froth turned a sickening gray.

"I have your brother," the river mocked her.

"No," she cried, "give him back to me!"

"The child is mine now," the river said, and it began to laugh, cackling in the voice of an old hag.

"No," Autumn Dawn cried again.

Then, the roiling waves turned into arms and they were holding something.

"Autumn, help me," Coyote Boy cried from the top of the cold, dark arm waves.

"I'm coming, little brother, wait . . . ."

Autumn Dawn stumbled down the riverbank, falling on a downed limb. A stab of pain pierced her knee as she felt blood trickle down her leg.

The waves folded themselves over the little boy. Coyote Boy let out one last cry of desperation before he disappeared.

Autumn screamed "No!" but the river ignored her. She had never felt so helpless.

Autumn Dawn startled herself awake. Coyote Boy was still folded in her own arms, not the River's. Autumn pulled him closer and for the first time allowed herself to weep. The feeling of helplessness from her dream seeped into her very bones. They would not survive. Her brother would starve or freeze, as would she eventually.

Or their enemies, the Bwaan, would find them. Tears ran down her cheeks as she waited for them to turn to ice like they had in her first dream of foretelling. Exhausted, she closed her eyes and drifted off to dream once more.

"It does not have to be a foretelling," a deep voice said to her. Autumn Dawn looked around. She didn't know where she was, could not make out who had spoken in the fog that surrounded her.

"It is only a foretelling if you are not strong in your heart."

The voice was louder, and now, through the fog, she was able to make out the shape of a tall dead pine tree. Was the tree talking to her?

"Do not leave this place," the voice commanded.

Suddenly, the fog cleared and it was as if springtime had conquered winter. The scents of flowers and wild berries surrounded her. The forest was lush and newly green, the sky a brilliant blue. The warm air embraced her and for the first time in days, she was not cold.

She looked closer at the tall dead pine.

There was something at the very top, a bird, perhaps. But it was like no bird she had ever seen.

It shimmered with a golden glow, and circling its head was an unearthly brightness. Suddenly, the creature flew off its branch and soared in her direction.

Autumn Dawn's heart quickened as the bird, which she now realized was an eagle, flew right up to her. Looking much like a great chief, the eagle was huge and resplendent with feathers of gold. The aura of piercing white light from around his bald head blinded her. It was he who had spoken.

"Do not fear this place," the eagle's low melodic voice repeated. "Stay."

A deer suddenly appeared out of nowhere, and Autumn Dawn's fear melted around her like springtime snow.

Autumn Dawn woke up the next morning, with a newfound confidence. "Wake up, Coyote Boy," she said as she shook her little brother.

The air was cold, but she paid it no mind. Good things were going to happen, she was sure of it now. The eagle had told her so.

"Are we going hunting right away, Autumn?" Coyote Boy asked as he sat up and rubbed his sleepy eyes.

"Yes," Autumn began, then reconsidered. "But first we will set snares here. For when we come back tonight."

"What if we don't come back tonight?" her little brother asked, fully awake now.

"We will. We shall find a deer today and return tonight triumphant with food to stuff our bellies and hides that will keep us warm."

She smiled at him and pulled him up. "But first, little one, you must tell me again all you know about hunting the deer. Especially the place we must strike him to make sure the kill is quick and painless."

Coyote Boy frowned at her. "How do you know we'll find one close enough to bring it back here tonight, Sister?"

"I know, Little Brother. Eagle came to me in a dream last night. He told me to stay here. I believe it was a true vision and not just a trickster's dream." Autumn looked up into the sky. The morning was cool, but the sky was clear and fine, as in her dream. There would be no mud to contend with this day.

"You had a vision, Sister?" Coyote Boy asked, his voice full of awe.

"Yes, I believe so. We must stay close to this place and look for the deer. He will come. I am sure of it."

She stood up and began searching the ground.

"Help me gather what we need to set the snares, little one. We will build a shelter here, also. Tonight we will have a feast."

Coyote Boy followed her. "But I will not eat unless we have found a deer, Sister," her brother said defiantly.

A frown started on her face but quickly changed into a smile. "Agreed, Brother. Now, help me gather some roots for snares."

But the deer did not show itself to Autumn Dawn that day.

Or the next.

Chapter Six

It was the afternoon of the third day after Autumn Dawn's vision. A light snow had fallen during the night. Autumn's eyes played tricks on her as she stumbled through the woods searching for tracks that were not there. Coyote Boy walked a little ways in front of her, looking more like a ghost than a boy.

Suddenly, he crumpled to the ground. Autumn was by his side in a heartbeat.

"Little Brother, what is it?" she asked. His eyes were closed, but he didn't seem to be asleep. Autumn shook him gently.

Coyote Boy's eyes opened half way. "Sister?" he asked as if he wasn't sure who she was.

"You are weak from hunger. I'm taking you back to the lodge, and you are going to eat."

He did not argue.

They had snared a bird and rabbit the past two days while out hunting, but she and Coyote Boy had eaten none of it because of the fast. Her weakness was great, but she hoped she could fast longer still. When she was twelve years old, her dream fast had lasted eight days.

Grandfather had needed to carry her home from her dreaming place in the forest, but she had been proud of herself.

Coyote Boy, however, was young. Little children did not fast as long as the older ones. She must make him eat today.

When they finally returned to their little lodge by the rushing river, Autumn Dawn herself nearly fainted with exhaustion. She slid Coyote Boy onto the shelter floor and immediately attended to restarting their meager fire.

While Coyote Boy ate, Autumn drank some water but ate no meat. She picked up the soft-furred rabbit skins she had collected and laid them out on the lodge floor. They would make a fine lining for deerskin moccasins. If they found a deer.

"Do you think your vision dream was wrong, Autumn?" Coyote Boy asked.

His doubts were as great as her own. Maybe the dream had been a trick after all. "I . . . do not think so," she said hesitantly. She wanted to believe in the vision. She wanted to believe the eagle. If she could not believe in the dream vision, there was nothing left.

She looked at her brother with new resolve. "The vision was a true one, Brother. Do you feel strong enough to go deer tracking again?"

Coyote Boy had finished his meal of rabbit meat. "Yes, Sister." He smiled at her.

"Then let's go right now, while we still have some light. I feel stronger too."

So, they left the campsite and followed a different path, leading off into the woods. More snow had fallen. Autumn Dawn hoped she would soon see fresh tracks in the old trail. The Wild Rice Moon was not long passed, but winter seemed to be coming early this year. Autumn was almost getting used to being cold. She could not remember the last time she felt really warm.

Crash! She walked right into Coyote Boy whom she hadn't noticed had stopped in the trail. Both of them went sprawling to the ground.

"Little Brother, what are you doing?" she asked, as she sat up, brushing snow off herself.

Coyote Boy scrambled to his feet. "Autumn, look!" He pointed to the ground.

There, just off the trail, were the fresh imprints of a deer's hooves.

"What a good little hunter you are, Brother!" With new energy she picked him up and spun herself around in a circle. Then she whispered, "The deer cannot be far from here. These are very fresh tracks." She set him back down.

Coyote Boy looked up at her, a question in his eyes.

"You will lead us, Brother. You were the first one to find the tracks."

Coyote Boy grinned with delight. She knew how much he wanted to be a man. Autumn Dawn felt her heart tighten, and a lump grew in her throat. He was so little to be so brave. She wanted to hug him again, but instead she simply nodded to him, as if to say, "Lead the way."

Coyote Boy moved with great care, slowly making his way down the path ahead of her. Autumn ran her fingers over the sturdy hickory bow she carried, reassuring herself that it was still there. She looked beyond her brother, hoping any minute to see the deer.

Then, suddenly, it was there. As if an apparition, the deer seemed to materialize out of nowhere, his tan coat showing up easily against the whitened forest. His antlers, huge and striking, moved gently from side to side as the deer foraged for food.

Autumn Dawn stopped walking. Coyote Boy did the same. The deer continued to look for greenery on the forest floor. He was an old buck and likely would not survive the winter.

Autumn checked the wind direction and realized it was coming straight at them from the direction of the deer. Their human scent would not reach the animal. Unless he looked right at them, he would not even know they were there.

Quietly, Autumn took an arrow from her belt. The deer kept his head down, nuzzling the ground in search of food.

"Caw, caw!" A crow let out a cry, high above from his perch in a tree.

The deer, startled by the sound, ran. Autumn Dawn's whole body tensed with frustration. "Stupid crow," she hissed as she and Coyote Boy took off after the deer.

They stayed close, but not too close behind the animal, avoiding branches that might snap and further alarm the deer. After a while, the animal slowed to a walk. When the old buck finally stopped, Autumn Dawn also stopped, well behind him. The deer looked nervously from side to side, ears twitching.

Autumn and Coyote Boy stood perfectly still. Then, the deer began calmly chewing on the bark of a tree. He seemed oblivious to their presence.

Autumn placed an arrow in her bow. Clearing her mind of all else, she closed her eyes and pictured the deer, gnawing peacefully on tree bark that would not sustain him for the coming harsh winter. Through the arrow, she would join with the deer in the instant of death. The deer would sacrifice itself for her sake and that of her little brother's.

Autumn opened her eyes and was not surprised to see the deer, turned toward her now, looking right at her. Autumn knew that life only comes of death. For that instant, she felt that the deer knew it too: both hunter and hunted, aware of what was expected of them.

Autumn Dawn took aim just above the deer's front leg, as Coyote Boy had instructed.

The arrow pierced the heart of the animal, swift and true. The deer let out a soft moan; to Autumn it sounded like a last thanksgiving for a quick end with little pain.

Autumn put her hand on Coyote Boy's shoulder and led him to the deer's side. She knelt down next to the creature who had given his life so they might live. His eyes still shone with a faint glimmer of life.

"*Miigwech.* Thank you, Brother Deer. Journey well to the land of the spirits." She handed Coyote Boy the last of her tobacco, and they both sprinkled it on the bloodstained snow.

The glimmer disappeared from the animal's eyes. Autumn Dawn Shines on Leaf reached for her brother and wept bittersweet tears.

Chapter Seven

Autumn Dawn sang again. She sang while she scraped the deerskin and tanned it over the fire. She sang while she cut the hide into pieces with her knife. She sang while she fashioned the bone and sinew into awl and thread, for sewing warm hand and foot coverings. Autumn would let no part of the deer go to waste.

The awl was made from a small pointed bone that needed just a little more sharpening with a jagged stone to make it a useful tool. With the sharp bone, she could punch holes in the hide. Then, using sinew as thread, she sewed the pieces together. She thanked the Great Spirit and Eagle for bringing them the gift of the deer.

The meat from the deer was sweet and filling. But Autumn found that after her fasting, she could not eat as much as she once could.

The meat gave Coyote Boy more energy than ever. It pleased Autumn Dawn to see him so happy and well fed. She decided they would stay here, in the camp by the rushing river, for the winter.

The first thing she did was to make a sapling framework for a proper wigwam. She chose a site close to the river's edge, within view of the waters but protected from prevailing winds by a thick cluster of pine trees.

Next, she made mats from the long grassy leaves of cattails that grew so abundantly in a marsh area a short walk downriver. The woven mats would help to insulate the wigwam against cold winter storms sweeping down from the north.

Finally, she covered the lodge, except for the smoke hole, with birchbark. Heavy rocks tied to string and placed over the roof held the sheets of birchbark down. The string she made herself from the inner bark of the basswood tree.

The weather remained fine and there were no harsh winds to interrupt her work. Autumn was sure Eagle had blessed them.

Next, she fashioned two pair of crude snowshoes for herself and Coyote Boy. Like the tanned hide, they weren't as finely crafted as her mother would have made them, but the worst of winter was coming soon and she had much to do before the first real blizzard. The deer meat might last through the cold months if they supplemented it with small animals caught in snares. In the spring, when travel would be easier, they would resume their search for distant relatives.

"Autumn, look! It is the eagle." Excited, Coyote Boy came running up to her as she sat outside the wigwam, constructing a small *makak*, a birchbark container.

It was a fine winter's day. The moon had traveled one complete path since they had killed the deer.

Autumn Dawn looked up, shading her eyes. "Indeed, Little One, it is Eagle. Perhaps he has come to join our feast."

Then she returned to her handwork. But as she pulled the strong thread of a peeled root tight, closing the seam on the small basket, she had the feeling of being watched. Quickly she glanced behind her and all around their campsite. But there was no one there—only Coyote Boy, making a snow-snake track in the freshly fallen snow.

A feeling of unease crept over her. Autumn Dawn looked up, searching for the eagle again. As if knowing her thoughts, Eagle swept down toward her—just as he had done in her vision. Close now, closer than ever before, he hovered, his feathers reflecting the light of the bright winter sun.

Then, as quickly as he'd come, he was gone. Autumn Dawn watched him fly swiftly away—headed northwest.

Her stomach sank within her. Could the eagle want her to follow him yet again? Surely not. They were safe and warm here. They would have plenty to eat. Traveling now, when the winds of winter were sure to bring frigid air, could be deadly. Besides, moving west would bring them closer to the disputed grounds where she might run into their enemies, the Bwaan.

No, Eagle could not have wanted her to follow. Perhaps he was just sending a greeting. Autumn Dawn put all thoughts of the great bird out of her mind.

But when Eagle returned the next day and the next, Autumn Dawn could no longer ignore him. Even Coyote Boy noticed.

"Autumn, why does Eagle fly so close every day? Have you had another vision? Are we supposed to follow him?"

She wished Coyote Boy were not quite so perceptive. She snapped at him, "I have had no vision, and I have no intention of following him."

Autumn Dawn got up from her place next to their outdoor fire and went into the wigwam. She knew her tone had been too harsh with her brother, but she couldn't help it. To leave now would be suicide. Why must the eagle persist in his attempts to lead her still farther north?

She looked around their lodge. It was small, and their belongings meager, but the wigwam was warm and would keep them safe through the winter. Why should they leave this place? Was Eagle not the one that had appeared to her in a vision, telling her to stay here?

Autumn tried to busy herself with tasks that would take her mind off Eagle, but the rest of the evening, the image of his great winged form flying off to the northwest haunted her. Later, as she lay in the dark, listening to Coyote Boy's even, contented breathing, she wondered again the reason for Eagle's persistent visits.

Sometime after she had fallen asleep, Autumn Dawn

woke up suddenly. Something had awakened her, a sound perhaps. At first she thought it might be a chorus of birds, but quickly realized birds would not be singing so late at night. This sound was of no wild animal she knew. No, as she sat up and listened closer, she knew it could only be the voices of men, raised in song:

"Passant par Paris, pour y vider bouteille . . ."

It was men, all right—French traders singing in the night. They were camped not far away, on the other side of the rushing river . . . probably on a sandy shore near the cattail marsh. They sounded as if they were drinking. So this is why the eagle wanted her to move.

Her people had traded with the French, and many were friendly. Little Dove, her cousin, had even married one. But it was contact with the traders that some believed had brought the illness on her people. Maybe that why Eagle wanted her to avoid these particular white men. She looked over at her brother, sleeping so peacefully. Should she wake Coyote Boy, so they could leave now? No, they must wait until morning, when the men would likely be sleeping off their liquor.

Autumn Dawn realized she had made a decision. She would sleep no more that night. Instead, she reached out, found her belt and took out her knife. Holding the handle firmly in her hand, she would remain, alert and awake, watching over her little brother.

Chapter Eight

Early the next morning, as the first rays of dawn crept into their wigwam, Autumn startled awake from an unwanted nap. She had tried not to sleep all night, intending to leave at first light, but she had dozed off, against her will.

Voices snapped her awake. Quietly, she moved over to the door of their wigwam and pulled the flap aside. The Frenchmen were upriver, a short distance from her campsite, loading their canoes, getting ready to leave. It was too late for her to pack up now. They would see or hear her for sure. Her only hope was that the pine trees that surrounded her shelter would hide their wigwam from the men as they passed by in their canoes. There was nothing else to do.

"Sister?" Coyote Boy's voice broke the silence.

"Shush," she whispered, as she quickly went to his side and put her hand over his mouth. "Do not make a sound. There are white men near."

Coyote Boy nodded his head and she released her hand.

Splash! The trader's canoe went into the water. Autumn held her breath. *Oh, Great Spirit, please let them pass us by. Spare my little brother the white man's disease.*

She and her brother sat perfectly still as they heard the canoe coming nearer and nearer. Each time the men's paddles hit the water, Autumn Dawn knew they were that much closer to her wigwam. She did not dare to look out the door flap. She did not breathe.

Then, in what seemed like a whole day, but could have only been a moment, the men passed by. Coyote Boy looked up at her, eyes wide.

"I think it is all right, Brother. They did not see us."

But was it really all right? Eagle had been circling for three days. Did he want them to move? Were there more white men nearby?

Maybe Eagle had been circling simply to find fish in the river. Once again, Autumn Dawn put all thoughts of the eagle, and moving, out of her mind.

The day turned out to be one of those pleasant winter days when the sun shines as if on fire, and the coldest winds have not yet swooped down from the north. Coyote Boy entertained himself playing snow-snake on the path next to the river. After taking his time to select just the right small branch, then carefully peeling off bark and removing any stubs that might keep it from sliding well, he spent much of the rest of the day sliding his snow-snake down the path, time after time.

As he made up his own games, he talked to himself cheerfully.

Watching him, she felt she had made the right decision. He was happy and well fed. They had all they needed here. Still, Autumn kept a wary eye out for more white men. She did not see Eagle all day, and this she took to mean she had misinterpreted his visits. Indeed, he had probably only been fishing.

But sometime during the night, Autumn Dawn awoke startled—once again to the sound of voices. Closer than the Frenchmen had been, these voices spoke a language unknown to her.

Autumn lay frightened, clutching her knife. At least she had known enough French to figure out that the earlier party of men had been singing a merry drinking song. This new language was dangerous because she did not understand it. What were they talking about? Were they plotting to attack her shelter?

They were close and getting closer. Should she try to run with Coyote Boy? No, that would be impossible. The men would hear them for sure. The voices were too close.

Crack! Not far away, a tree branch snapped. Autumn grabbed Coyote Boy and sat up.

"What is happening?" he asked sleepily.

"Hush, Little Brother."

Suddenly, the voices outside were silent, but Autumn Dawn could still hear their footfalls. Then, the voices began again, but this time they were mere whispers.

They must have seen the wigwam.

Autumn Dawn clutched the knife firmly in her hand, even as she held tightly to Coyote Boy. The footfalls stopped. She knew they were right outside.

Autumn watched the deerskin door flap. Even in the cool night air, beads of sweat erupted on her forehead.

Then, a hand pushed aside the flap and a man's face appeared. When he saw Autumn Dawn, he quickly disappeared, letting the buckskin fall back into place. In the firelight, she could see it had been the face of a white man.

Not a Bwaan warrior. She let out a tiny bit of the breath she was holding.

A gruff voice said something, but Autumn could not understand a word of the language.

Another softer voice replied.

Gruff Voice said something again. All at once the buckskin was pushed aside, and three men crowded into her small shelter. For a moment they didn't say anything.

Autumn used that moment to assess her position. The man in the middle was very large. And there was no way to slip past him and the other two, packed together shoulder to shoulder just inside the wigwam doorway. Any escape was blocked.

The other two men were smaller than the large man in the middle, but even so, she and Coyote Boy were no match for three grown men. If indeed they were a threat, she would have to get out of this by her wits rather than her physical strength.

In the firelight, she studied their faces for signs of the trader's illness. They all looked healthy enough. That was little comfort, though, as some people in her band had looked healthy one day and were dead the next.

The man on the left leaned toward her with eyebrows raised and said something. He was the soft-voiced one. It seemed like he was asking her a question. These white men looked similar to the French she had known, but their language was incomprehensible. Soft Voice moved and talked like a kindly person, but just the same, she wasn't about to trust any of them.

Now Gruff Voice and Soft Voice were talking to each other. The man on the right remained silent, examining her and Coyote Boy. Gruff Voice sounded impatient.

Just like a white man, Autumn thought. They were always impatient, her father had once said to her.

Soft Voice took a step closer to Autumn. Her whole body tensed up. She held the knife firmly in her hand.

". . . trade . . . ?"

He was attempting to speak an Indian language, but it wasn't hers. He must have learned it from people far to the east. He seemed friendly enough, but without the gestures another Indian would have used, she couldn't understand most of what he spoke. She thought she had heard the word *trade*, though.

"Who are you?" she asked in her own language.

The men looked at each other. Then, Soft Voice put his hand out. He said something again, in that strange Indian language. He seemed to want her to come with them.

Autumn did not completely understand, but she knew she didn't want to take his hand. She drew away from him.

Gruff Voice said something in the men's own foreign tongue. He was getting impatient again.

Autumn Dawn did not trust him. She wanted to trust Soft Voice but she didn't dare.

The two men argued some more. The third man still did not speak. Autumn wondered if he were mute.

"What are they saying, Autumn?" Coyote Boy wriggled out of her tight grasp and looked up at her.

She grabbed him again. "I am not sure. I think they want to trade with us."

If they were traders, like the French, would she tell them where her people were, if she knew? No, she would not. She would be putting her people in danger. It was strangers that had brought the illness on her people. Besides, what if they wanted something other than trade?

The men stopped arguing. Soft Voice moved closer to Autumn. Quickly, she pointed her knife at him. She was no match for the three of them, but she would not go with them without a fight.

The man stopped and looked at her, confusion on his face. Then, he seemed to get an idea.

"Can you tell us where your people are?" This time he spoke in French. Autumn had learned just a little of that language from her cousin's mate, but she had not spoken it in a long time.

"No, I do not know where my people are," she replied in the best French she could remember.

"We are Englishmen. We have come to trade with your people."

The language was coming back to her now. And something else came back to her. She remembered listening to her cousin's mate talk about the English—how they had moved into the Frenchmen's trading territory and were trying to take it over. They were the Frenchmen's enemy.

Autumn knew no Englishmen. But if they were her cousin's enemy, then they were her enemy as well.

"I have nothing to trade here," she answered, pointing the knife at him.

He looked at her with what she thought was concern. "Do you need help? Are you lost?"

She was tempted to let the man help her. She was so tired of searching. Tired of being the only one taking care of her brother. Tired of being an adult.

But no, she must not trust them.

She would find her people on her own. "No, I am not lost. Go now," she said, as firmly as she could, although her insides were trembling.

Gruff Voice made a derisive sound and quickly left the shelter. The mute one followed. Soft Voice hesitated, looking at her with puzzlement. Autumn continued to hold her knife out in front of her. Finally Soft Voice sighed and left.

Autumn let out the breath she had been holding.

"Who were those men?" Coyote Boy asked.

"I do not know, Little Brother, but I am glad they are gone," she said as she lay down her knife.

Coyote Boy lay down as well. As Autumn Dawn looked at him, a tugging fear played around her heart. But she had decided. "Tomorrow, we shall follow the eagle. Perhaps we will find our own people at last," she reassured him. And not the Bwaan, she asked silently of the Great Spirit.

"You mean we have to leave this place by the river?" Disappointment filled her brother's voice.

"I am afraid so, Little One. We must find our people." But Autumn Dawn Shines on Leaf had little confidence in her own words.

Chapter Nine

"But you said we would stay here for the winter,"
Coyote Boy complained the next morning, when Autumn
Dawn reminded him they must move on.

"It is not safe here anymore, Brother." But she knew
it might not be safe further west either. That was the
land of the Bwaan.

"Still, I do not want to go." He was being especially
stubborn this morning.

"Have you forgotten it was the white men who
brought us the terrible sickness? Eagle leads us. We
must follow." She put her hand on his shoulder, but
Coyote Boy would not look up at her.

"Remember the other day when you saw the eagle?"

"Yes . . ." He sounded as if he did not want to remember.

"You asked me if I thought he wanted us to move."

"That did not mean I *wanted* to move." Coyote Boy
said defiantly. "I like it here."

Autumn Dawn looked at him, her frustration tempt-
ing to boil over. They were outside the wigwam, and she

had asked him to help her roll up the cattail mats that they would need to take with them.

"You do not have a choice, Brother. It is dangerous here."

Coyote Boy sat down on the frosted ground. He said nothing, but his look dared her to make him budge.

She felt like grabbing him and shaking some sense into him. But, no, Mother would not do that. What *would* Mother do? Autumn Dawn thought a moment, and then she knew.

Silently she went about her work, taking the mats off the walls of the wigwam, and rolling them up. She would leave the birchbark roof behind. Next, she gathered all the deer meat she had dried and some of the fresh. Luckily, it was cold enough to keep the meat frozen. Then, she gathered the precious buckskin she had tanned and rolled it up. All the while she worked, she said nothing to her brother.

Coyote Boy simply sat, looking at the ground, making patterns with his fingers in the frost. When Autumn was finally ready to leave, she turned to him. "I am leaving now." She hoisted her pack on her back and headed off to the northwest.

As she walked, she resisted the temptation to look behind her. Was he there? Would he follow her? She could not just leave him—it was too dangerous. Maybe this was a bad idea. Maybe she should have grabbed him and dragged him along.

Then, she heard a branch break behind her. Without a glance back, she said, "It is dangerous for one to make so much noise in the woods."

Coyote Boy didn't respond, but she knew he was there.

The day was cold, but at least there was no snow to blind their path. However, Autumn Dawn's load wore heavily on her after walking only a short distance. Finally, Coyote Boy spoke up.

"Autumn, I will help carry something."

She looked back at him and stopped. "Very well. Here, take these," she said as she handed him a parcel of dried meat.

"I can take more," he said, as if in apology for his earlier behavior.

She said nothing, but handed him a roll of mats as well. She knew that was about all a six-year-old could handle.

Autumn wondered if the French or English men might have built a new trading post nearby. When traders were seen traveling through her people's territory, they were usually either on their way to a post or to an Indian settlement.

But this early in the season, it was unlikely that the Indians would have many skins to trade. The best skins came later, from hunts deep into the cold moons of winter—when the animals wore their most luxurious coats of thick fur.

So the two groups of white men were probably each on their way to their winter quarters. She wondered where those posts were. She and her brother must be sure to avoid other white men who might be traveling through the area as well.

As the day wore on and the temperature grew colder, Autumn tried to comfort herself with the hope that if traders were in the area, relatives of hers might be also.

A chilling thought occurred to her. Those men could be here to trade with the Bwaan. How was she to avoid both the white men and the Bwaan? She dismissed the question and kept a steady pace, with Coyote Boy close on her heels. There was no easy answer.

That night, as they set up camp, the air grew colder. They were glad they had their deerskin now. With the cattail mats, Autumn set up a temporary shelter. But it would still be a cold night. She didn't want to take the time to build a decent wigwam, since they were only going to be here one night.

And one night was all they could afford to stay. They weren't yet far enough away from the white men to be safe.

Winter showed itself in full force the next day, as an icy wind from the north brought lower temperatures. Before heading into it, Autumn Dawn wrapped a piece of deer hide around Coyote Boy's face to protect him. With his eyes peering out from above the mask, he looked like a raccoon.

Then, she fastened a similar piece around her own nose. It hung down to cover her mouth, leaving her own eyes free to see ahead.

Why did the white men have to show up? She and Coyote Boy had been safe and warm in the wigwam by the river. Ordinarily, her people would not venture out from their lodges to travel great distances in the winter, unless there was a shortage of animals to hunt. But now, she and her small brother must plunge ahead, following Eagle's path directly into the cold wind.

Perhaps he leads us to our people, she thought. She knew there were other Anishinaabe living to the north and west. But how far?

And she knew too well, the Bwaan also lived somewhere to the west.

When the sun was high in the sky, Autumn and her brother stopped to eat. They found shelter in a thick stand of pines, on the banks of a frozen creek. Facing away from the wind and chewing on a piece of dried deer meat, Autumn considered setting up camp right there. Coyote Boy was shivering. They needed a fire. They hadn't gone far enough, though. The white men could be near by. The white men—and their disease.

"Look, Sister, there is Eagle." Coyote Boy pointed to the sky.

There he was, circling high above, as if waiting for them to move on again. Once again, Eagle would help her make her decision.

"He wants us to follow, Coyote Boy," Autumn said with a sigh. *I think Eagle demands too much of us*, she thought. She stood up. "Let us go now, Little Brother. Perhaps there are good things in store for us ahead." She tried to smile as he looked up at her.

Much later, as the merciless wind bit at them, Autumn Dawn could no longer see the eagle. No longer could she even see the sky. The wind was accompanied by an icy snow that lashed at her face, seeking the few places where her flesh was bare.

After Coyote Boy tripped for the third time, Autumn knew they had to stop. She looked around and spotted a stand of saplings, clustered next to a young but sturdy-looking birch tree. It was perfect for a shelter.

"We will camp here for the night. The snow is too blinding to see our way."

Although he had not complained, Coyote Boy looked relieved.

"You are a brave little coyote," she said as she put her arm around him, squeezing his shoulder gently.

They quickly unrolled the cattail mats and strung them over the small trees. In no time, they had a make-shift shelter built—not as sturdy as the wigwam by the river, but it would do for one night.

Later, as she lay by the fire, after Coyote Boy had fallen asleep, Autumn Dawn heard the lonely cry of a wolf. As she drew in a breath, she heard an answer from what sounded like a large pack of wolves.

She knew *maiingan*, Brother Wolf, would not harm a human, unless it were starving. It was too early in winter for that.

Still, on this night, the animal's cry sent chills down Autumn's spine.

Sometime later in the midst of the darkness, Autumn woke up to a wailing sound. At first she thought it was the wolves again. But as her head cleared of sleep, she realized it was the wind. It had picked up in intensity, and ghostly blasts of snow were being forced in through the chinks in her temporary shelter. She tried to ignore the howling and whistling, but its chilling fingers were everywhere.

Crack!

Autumn heard the crunch of a large tree breaking.

In the next instant one entire wall of her shelter came crashing down around her—the wall closest to Coyote Boy. She reached over to try to protect him, but it was too late. The young birch had snapped, causing Coyote Boy's part of the small shelter to fall in on top of him.

Her brother woke with a start. For a moment he didn't say anything. Then he screamed.

"Autumn!"

"Little Brother, you will be all right," she said, keeping her voice calm as she struggled to her knees and tried to pull aside the fallen mats. Panic was beginning to form in the pit of her stomach. She'd been sleeping next to Coyote Boy, and it amazed her that the tree hadn't hit her as well.

The birch had fallen on Coyote Boy's left leg. He cried out with every move she made, but still she could not lift the tree. Something was holding it down.

The wind roared in Autumn Dawn's ears and threw icy pellets of snow at her as she tried to see what was wrong. Finally able to focus her eyes, she realized to her horror what had happened. A full-grown towering pine, once a majestic member of the forest, had toppled under the force of the wind. As it fell in their direction, it had taken down all of the brush and young trees that fought for growth underneath it. The birch that had fallen on Coyote Boy's leg was itself trapped under the much larger tree.

For a moment she just stared in the darkness at the looming outline of the large, downed tree. Then, a shiver went through her whole body as she realized how close to disaster they had come. If the giant pine tree had fallen just a few feet closer, they both would have been killed. She uttered a quick thanks to the Great Spirit for sparing their lives.

"Help me!" Coyote Boy wailed.

She turned back to her brother and pulled out

her knife. It was small, meant for simple uses, but it was her only sharp tool. The downed birch was larger than she could put her two hands around, but this was the only answer. Controlling the shaking that threatened to overwhelm her, Autumn Dawn carefully began sawing on the young birch that held her brother's leg captive.

With each motion of her arm Coyote Boy winced, but he no longer cried out. He was trying to be so grown-up. "Some day you will be a great warrior, Little Brother," Autumn said. "You are brave and not afraid of pain."

His voice was small. "I do not like pain, though."

"No one does." Autumn reminded him.

She worked quietly for a while, then had an idea. "How about if I sing you a song?" she asked. Autumn knew how much he enjoyed her singing and perhaps it would distract him from the pain.

"I would like that," he answered.

"Which song would you like?"

Coyote Boy shrugged, as if stifling a cry.

"How about the dog song? You know, the fishermen and the good giant with the dog who outsmarts the evil *wiindigoo*?"

Coyote Boy nodded. It was one of his favorites.

So, Autumn Dawn sang the song of the fishermen. She sang while the wind whistled around her. She sang while the snow pelted her face with icy needles. She sang while she sawed the tree until her fingers ached so much she thought they would never straighten out again. By the time she was through, her voice was but a whisper. She lost count of all the verses she'd made up to keep her brother's mind off his pain. The blizzard still howled all around them, and they were both covered with a dusting of icy snow.

When she finally lifted the birch off her brother's leg, he cried in pain. Quickly, she built a fire from the glowing coals left from the evening before, adding small sticks of wood until they blazed into flame. In the dim firelight, she was not pleased with what she saw. Coyote Boy's shin was swollen and, she could see through a tear in his leggings, was discoloring quickly. The bone might be fractured. She wouldn't know for sure until she examined it.

"Coyote Boy, I will need you to be brave once again."

He simply nodded.

"I am going to have to touch the place on your leg that is injured. I will try to be careful, but this may hurt a little."

Ever so carefully, Autumn placed her hands on her brother's leg. He jumped slightly, but didn't cry out.

She pressed a little harder, and he let out a quiet moan. Then, she felt it—a slight fracture. Not a complete break, but enough that he shouldn't walk on it for a while.

Autumn Dawn drew her hands away and thought

about her supplies. She had a few medicines stored up, but she was not sure it would be enough. She would have to make him a birchbark cast. She could use the bark from this very tree that had fallen on him, but getting it off the trunk in cold weather would be difficult. She thought of a plan.

"I will have to move you away from the tree, little one, so I can rebuild our shelter. Your leg will hurt when I lift you. Can you be brave one more time?"

"Yes, sister."

Although his words were brave, she heard the pain in them. Autumn bit her lip to keep her own tears away.

Very carefully, she picked her brother up. He winced, but did not cry out. Gently, she set him down, away from the fallen tree but close to the fire.

Quickly, she added more wood to the glowing embers which had almost died out again. It was important to keep Coyote Boy warm. Next, she set the cut piece of birch log to warm by the fire. That would make it easier to peel off the bark. Then she went about pulling aside the fallen brush and broken tree limbs so she could put their shelter back together. She would make a sturdier shelter, a real wigwam, because they would have to stay here until Coyote Boy was healed enough to travel.

While the wind and snow howled around her, Autumn worked quickly. She'd never had to build a wigwam in a blizzard before. Her people always had them completed well before a dangerous storm arrived. Her fingers, already stiff from cutting the birch tree, ached with cold. She could not wear hand coverings, though, as they were too bulky to work in.

Much time passed before she finished. Her hands no longer ached; they were numb instead. She crouched down next to the fire. She had built the wigwam around her brother and the fire—they were both in the middle of the shelter now. In the blizzard, if too much snow came in the smoke hole, she would be forced to put the fire out and cover the hole, and try to keep warm another way.

She pulled on the rabbit fur-mittens she had made when they had camped by the river. Watching the meager fire, she wondered: if she had been alone, would she have given up by now? Just let herself die in these woods?

It was a stupid question. If she didn't have a brother, she might still be back at camp, taking care of Mother. Then, perhaps, she too would have fallen ill to the sickness. Perhaps she would even now be walking with her ancestors in the next world.

Autumn Dawn shivered. Was Mother there already, in the Spirit world? So many others she had known and loved were. Her thoughts turned to White Otter. Just a few moons ago, they had been the best of friends.

Now . . . suddenly she was overwhelmed with a grief so raw it could not be denied. She had tried to be so strong for Coyote Boy. But now her heart felt as if it would break in pieces like lake ice in the spring. Her body crumpled down into the snowy dirt floor and she gave herself up to the tears.

Autumn Dawn wept. She wept for all those she had loved and lost to the white man's illness. Why, Great Spirit, must so many die? Have my people displeased you so? Her body shook with uncontrollable sobs. Autumn thought she would never stop weeping.

When finally her tears came to an end, the anguish in her heart had loosened its grip. She felt sad, but at peace. If her people had displeased the Great Spirit, she must help turn things right again. She must pay close attention to his messages. She must be true to the signs, in dreams and in the waking hours.

"It will be all right, Autumn." Coyote Boy's voice startled her.

How long had he been awake? How long had he heard her weep?

"Eagle will help us."

Fresh sobs started, but this time she did not hide them as she reached out to her brother.

"You are wise for your age, Coyote Boy," she said as she hugged him gently. He was all she had left—and a worthy companion he was. "Thank you for being so brave."

Exhausted, she lay down beside him and closed her eyes. In another moment she was asleep.

Chapter Ten

Autumn Dawn did not sleep long though. Even in her dream state she knew she must tend to Coyote Boy's wound. Only a few short moments later, she woke up with a start. Was it her imagination, or had the wind started to die down?

Coyote Boy was still awake. She shook her head to rouse herself. "You shouldn't have let me fall asleep, Little Brother."

"I'm all right, Autumn."

"I must make a poultice for your break." She took off her mittens and reached for her medicine bag. She took out the roots of the spikenard and wild-ginger plants that she had collected at the beginning of their journey. They were dried now and just right for mashing. Carefully, Autumn Dawn worked the roots with her fingers until they were pulverized.

She put snow in the stomach of the deer she had slain, and hung it over the fire to heat. She would wash Coyote Boy's wound with the warm water.

Finally, everything was prepared.

"I am going to wash your leg now, Little One. It will hurt a bit."

As gently as she could, Autumn washed Coyote Boy's shin. He grimaced with pain, but said nothing. Next she rubbed deer grease on the wound and finally applied the poultice of roots. It was a messy mash, held together by a small piece of buckskin. "You will have to hold this on your leg while I peel bark for the cast."

Autumn Dawn reached for the birch log. She took out her knife and tried to peel the bark away. But her plan to warm up the log had not worked. The sap was still frozen to the innards of the tree, and the bark would not easily yield to her knife.

Autumn's fingers felt as if they would break off as she struggled with the bark. When she did manage to get a piece of bark off, it was much too small to be of any use to her.

But she did not give up. After what seemed like forever, surrounded by many discarded scraps of curling bark, Autumn finally had two good-sized sheets of birchbark, suitable for a cast. She put the scraps aside. Nothing must be wasted. They would make excellent tinder later.

"I finally have enough bark, Little One." His eyes were closed and he didn't answer. She could see he was not asleep though, as he still held the poultice of mashed roots on his shin.

"I'm going to add some warm water to make that nice and soft, Brother." Autumn moved his hand away from his leg. "This should not hurt."

Coyote Boy opened his eyes just a little, warily, but also curious.

Autumn Dawn poured a small amount of warm water over the poultice. Next she heated the birchbark and bent it to the proper shape to fit over his leg. This was more difficult. As she began pressing the birchbark in place, Coyote Boy flinched.

"I am sorry, but you must try to lie very still."

Carefully, she patted the two warm, hard rolls of birchbark in place. In a moment, she was through. "You must keep that leg very straight and still." She tied a piece of basswood twine around his leg to keep the cast in place. She squeezed his small hand and moved closer to the fire.

"I will try to be still, Autumn."

While warming her stiff fingers over the fire, she began to make plans. They still had plenty of meat. They could stay here until spring, once she made sure this new wigwam was as sturdy as the one they had left behind on the river. But would Eagle let them? Or would they soon see Eagle swooping down out of the sky to lead them on yet another treacherous journey?

What would she do if he did so? Autumn Dawn didn't even have to think about the answer. Coyote Boy could not be moved for some time, particularly if infection set in. Even if it didn't, he wouldn't be walking for more than a moon.

Eagle would just have to wait.

Chapter Eleven

The weather cleared. Over the next week, Autumn Dawn's life settled into a comfortable pattern. Once again they had a warm shelter in a safe place. They had enough deer meat to last the winter, and now and then the snares yielded a bird or rabbit. Autumn longed to stay here until spring.

She checked Coyote Boy's wound daily. To her relief, no infection had set in. When it came to illness or injury, she knew the basics, but Autumn was not trained to be a healer. Her gift, her mother had often said, was her voice. Lately she felt like singing once again.

She sang as she trudged through the deep snow, thankful for her snowshoes. Made in haste, they weren't the most beautiful pair she'd ever seen, but they would do. The blizzard had dropped a great amount of snow, and it slowed her down. It did not matter, though. She was no longer in a hurry to get anywhere.

"Autumn, when will I be able to walk again?" Coyote Boy asked as she entered the wigwam with a fresh rabbit for roasting.

"Soon, Little One. I was just thinking of having you try to stand on your leg a little today, to build your strength up. Would you like to try?"

"Yes!"

"All right then, let us try."

Autumn Dawn laid the rabbit aside. She bent down and faced her brother. "Now, put both your arms around my neck, and I will help you stand up." Coyote Boy leaned forward and grasped her neck tightly. Autumn slid her hands under his arms and pulled him up. Then, letting go of his right arm, she supported his left side, the side of his injured leg.

"Put a little weight on it, just a little. . . ."

Coyote Boy gingerly straightened his injured leg and slowly let it touch the ground.

"Ouch," he said. "It's sore."

"Try stepping down a little harder." He straightened up.

"That's good. How does that feel?" she asked.

"Not so good, Autumn. Do you think I'll ever be able to walk again?"

She laughed. "Of course you will. Did you ever hear of any of our people who turned into a cripple from a simple broken leg?" She wasn't sure herself, but tried to sound as confident as she could.

"Well, I guess not. But it feels bad."

Autumn helped lower him back down to the ground. "It's healing just fine. You will be up and around in no time. I promise."

Coyote Boy frowned at her. "Promise?"

"You have my word."

Two weeks went by and Coyote Boy was able to hobble around the wigwam with a crutch he'd whittled from a branch. Watching him, Autumn Dawn felt her heart swell with pride. So brave, he rarely complained of pain. She was proud, too, that she had managed to take care of him and provide an adequate shelter for the two of them.

She had even tracked a deer! And every day now, the snares had something in them. She felt sure Eagle was watching over them, but she was glad she had not seen him for awhile.

Then one cold clear afternoon, as she made her way through a clearing, there he was. *Eagle.* At first when she saw him, she quickly looked away, afraid to believe it was him. Perhaps it was just a hawk circling above.

Then she heard a swooshing noise, and felt a great wind passing by her. Autumn Dawn looked up and the bird was so close his distinctive white head couldn't be denied. As before, he seemed to hover for a second, then he quickly took off, heading northwest.

At first, all Autumn could feel was anger. "Foolish Eagle," she cried out loud. "How do you expect me to follow you with an injured brother?"

She was glad her brother wasn't anywhere nearby to hear her outburst, but she wasn't sorry for it either. Coyote Boy was still limping. No one would be foolish enough to take him on such a journey. And why was it so important for her to get to the northwest?

Didn't Eagle know that if she strayed too far west, she might run into a hunting party of Bwaan? And the Bwaan were no friend of the Anishinaabe.

Eagle was unreasonable. She simply would ignore him.

"Sister! Look, I'm walking better today," Coyote Boy said as she entered the wigwam.

"Hmm, yes." She was still thinking of the eagle.

"Autumn, you are not looking," he said. "I can walk on my sore leg."

Dismissing the image of the eagle, Autumn forced herself to look at her brother. Small as he was, he was indeed standing straight on both legs.

"You are doing well, Brother. You are a fast healer." *That is good, for I fear Eagle has another journey in store for us.*

"Did you see Eagle today, Autumn?" Coyote Boy asked.

Her heart quickened. "Why do you ask?"

"When I was outside, I saw him. Do you think he will lead us somewhere else?"

Autumn didn't know what to say. Coyote Boy was too quick. She couldn't hide anything from him anymore.

"I do not know, Brother. I want you to heal more before we decide to move on. I hope Eagle can be patient."

Eagle came back each day. This time, Autumn Dawn waited a whole week before she made the decision to move on. Coyote Boy was healing fast, but still the journey would be hard for him. The cold would only irritate his injury, and she couldn't make a new wigwam every night. They'd be sleeping in rough shelters until they got to wherever Eagle was leading them.

Rather than loading them both down with packs—Coyote Boy could not carry much with his sore leg—Autumn built a roughly hewn sledge before they left. The runners were made from some long, curved branches, with their bark whittled off to make them as smooth as possible. The crosspieces were more branches, tied down in a zigzag pattern. Like the snowshoes, the sledge was not beautiful. But it worked and that was all that mattered.

The morning they set off was warm for mid-winter. There were a few clouds, but not enough to predict a storm. Autumn felt confident the day would go well.

But after watching Coyote Boy hobble along, leaning more and more on his crutch, she decided to stop soon. "It is time to rest." Her brother, who had not complained, looked relieved.

As they sat chewing on dried deer meat, Autumn got an idea. "Little Brother, I think I will put you on the sledge and pull you along. Then your leg will not tire so."

"I am not a weakling," he objected. "Only weaklings and old people have to ride on the sledge."

"Oh, but you will have an important job to do. You will have to hold our belongings and make sure they do not fall off."

Coyote Boy seemed to think about that. "But they are not falling off now. They are tied on, Autumn."

He was too smart for her. How was she going to get him to ride on the sledge without feeling like a weakling? Then, she had an idea.

"But I need you to be my look-out."

"Your look-out?"

"Yes. You will ride backward and make sure no Bwaan warriors are following us."

"Bwaan warriors?" Coyote Boy's eyes went wide.

"Yes. We are in Bwaan country now, and we must be careful." She wasn't sure that was true, but Autumn knew her brother would find the prospect of tricking one of their enemies exciting.

"Then I must be your look-out."

"You must."

But shortly after they set out, to her own surprise, Autumn saw snowshoe tracks. It gave her a sudden burst of hope, followed as quickly by a chilling doubt. Were they the tracks of her own people? Or of the Bwaan? She did not know. Coyote Boy had not noticed so she did not speak of it with him.

Her brother seemed to be enjoying himself, but Autumn Dawn found it difficult to pull him and all their belongings too. At least we have belongings, she thought.

Considering she'd started this journey with nothing but a knife and her medicine bag, they had done very well for themselves.

It was slow-going, pulling the sledge through the soft snow. When the afternoon sun began to settle on the horizon, Autumn stopped her endless pulling. As she let go of the pull-strap, her arm suddenly was struck with a sharp pain. It had been in one position too long.

"We will camp here for the night, Little Brother." She sighed as she helped him up off the sledge. She was so tired and her arms ached so, it was all she could do to put up a makeshift shelter. The stars were out though, and there was no wind, so she wasn't too fussy about their lodge.

The next day started out clear, but as the day wore on, clouds began to gather. A winter storm was moving in. Autumn used both her arms pulling the sledge, first the right one, then the left, then both, but still she could not stop the aching.

The wind picked up, and now they were walking right into it. Autumn began to think she couldn't pull her burden any farther, and when the snow began to fall in earnest, she was almost glad for the excuse to have to stop for the night.

But even as they began to build a shelter, it became clear to Autumn they had waited too long. Dark, tumbling clouds moved in fast on a howling wind that seemed almost unnatural. She had never seen a blizzard intensify so quickly. The wind snatched the branches from their very hands as they tried to construct a simple shelter. It was obvious that they had run out of time to finish. Autumn had to make a quick decision.

Her father had told her a story once of her great-grandfather who had been caught in a blizzard while on a hunting trip. Like today, the wind was too strong to fight against, and instead of making a wood lodge, he buried himself in the snow for the duration of the storm. The next morning, he was alive and well-insulated in his blanket of snow. Could she do that?

"Coyote Boy," she called through the storm. He was limping around, trying with no success to fasten some branches together.

He didn't reply.

"Coyote Boy," Autumn called louder, but the wind carried her words away.

Finally, she went to him and laid her hand on his shoulder.

He fell into the snow.

"I'm sorry, Little Brother. I didn't mean to knock you down."

"My leg, Autumn." He looked up at her with tears in his eyes. "It hurts too much to stand on. I wanted to help but . . ."

He began to cry.

Autumn knelt down next to him. "Do not cry, Little Brother, the tears will freeze on your face."

But he continued sobbing as if his heart would break. Autumn knew he must be in a lot of pain to weep so. She pulled him to her, wincing herself, as her arms, stiff from pulling the sledge, felt as if they might break also.

"It is all right. We cannot build a real shelter in this storm anyway. We will make ourselves a snow blanket instead."

He looked up at her. "A snow blanket?"

"Yes. Remember the story about great-grandfather and the snow blanket that saved his life?"

"Yes," Coyote Boy answered, wiping his tears away. "We are going to bury ourselves in snow?"

"Yes," Autumn answered with enthusiasm. "Surely, the snow will save our lives, just like it did great-grandfather's."

"The snow will be our friend," Coyote Boy said.

"The snow will be our friend," Autumn Dawn repeated, trying to convince herself it was true.

Chapter Twelve

"Will this be like the time we buried ourselves in sand at the Big Water, Autumn?" Coyote Boy asked, as Autumn Dawn led him over to a pine tree. The icy wind pummeled their backs, pushing them along.

"No," she answered. The wind wasn't quite so bad in the shelter of the tree. "See this drift?" Autumn pointed to a large drift that had already formed against the tree. "We will make a house out of it, Little Brother. The snowdrift will be our blanket."

Autumn Dawn got down on her hands and knees, trying to pack more snow around the drift to make it even bigger, but she had no success. The snow was too fluffy and dry. It would not pack.

Instead, she began carefully digging a small tunnel into the drift, just big enough for her and Coyote Boy to crawl into. Luckily, under the new, soft snow, the drift was made of older snow, well packed.

"We will make our own cave," she said, looking over her shoulder at Coyote Boy. The wind-driven snow lashed her face.

"Can I help?" he asked.

"You just sit still and rest your leg." She had to shout in order for him to hear her above the storm. "It will only get worse if you struggle around needlessly in the snow. Save your strength so you can crawl into our snow cave."

Autumn dug down deep, into the drift, clearing the snow from what would become the base of their snow cave. Soon she reached the blanket of soft pine needles at the bottom. These would be good insulation to keep them dry. However, they would need more.

After working for what seemed like a day, she stopped to rest. She was afraid that if she made the hole any bigger the whole drift would collapse, and they would be left with no shelter at all.

"Hand me a stick, Coyote Boy," she called to him through the wind. She watched him the whole time he searched, so as not to let him out of her sight. In weather like this, he could get lost in a heartbeat.

It took her brother a while to find a stick in the deep snow. When he did, she quickly used it to poke a hole through a wall of the snow cave for ventilation.

"Now, pull some branches off the pine tree. We will need them for our floor."

This task took Coyote Boy a lot longer, so while she waited, Autumn Dawn worked to smooth out the interior of the cave so he would have enough room to lie down without rubbing up against the walls.

She looked out often to make sure that Coyote Boy

was working on his task, pulling little branches from the low arms of the great pine tree swept down almost to the ground.

Finally, he handed her the pine boughs. He was covered with snow.

"Thank you." She quickly laid the boughs on the floor of the cave. "Brush the snow off yourself and come in, Little Brother. It's ready." She crawled out of the small hole and turned to him. "I want you to crawl in first." She smiled, encouraging him, even as a powerful gust of wind circled the tree and blasted into her.

Coyote Boy wiggled into the small shelter. "This is fun," he said, giggling as he made himself comfortable.

To him it was a game, but Autumn knew better. This game could have life-and-death consequences. She smiled at her brother anyway.

"There's no room for you." Coyote Boy looked out, worried.

"I will be fine. I will sit in the doorway of our cave to keep the wind out. The falling snow will pile up on me and make a real blanket, just like it did for Grandfather."

"I don't know, Sister . . . you might freeze out there."

Autumn Dawn looked west, the direction the storm was coming from. Icy snow blew into her hair and eyes. There was even snow in her mouth. It chilled her as it melted on her tongue.

"I will be fine. If Grandfather could do this, so can I."

But Autumn wondered if it were true. Could someone actually save himself by covering up with snow—or was that just a children's story Father had told them, to entertain them on a cold winter's night around a wigwam fire?

Father, look what has become of us now. Perhaps we would be better off in the spirit world with you.

But no sooner had she thought it than she regretted it. Father would not want her thinking so. He would want her to take care of her brother. The story Father told must be true—he did not tell falsehoods about such important matters. Autumn curled herself up in the entrance to the snow cave.

"It is warm in here, Autumn. I wish you could come all the way in."

"I am warm here, too, Little Brother. Do not worry so."

Coyote Boy was quiet then, and Autumn Dawn put her head down on her knees to keep the snow out of her face. She would not sleep, though.

"Autumn . . . ?" Coyote Boy said after only a little time had passed.

"Yes, Little Brother."

"I was just thinking about that time we played on the shore of the Big Water. Do you think we will get to do that again?"

"I'm sure we will, Brother. I am sure we will." Autumn's throat tightened around her reply. She remembered the summer day when they'd been fishing at the lake. She had been younger then. On the lakeshore there was abundant sand, and the two of them had buried each other in it, all except for their heads.

Mother had laughed at their childish play.

Autumn Dawn tried to smile, but panic was beginning to settle like a wooden stick ball in her stomach.

She could be a child no longer. Coyote Boy was quiet now, but she felt like screaming. He didn't realize how close to death they both were. If the snow failed to protect them . . .

Autumn shook off the panic. *I can't let Coyote Boy know that I am afraid.* If nothing else, he deserves to die in peace, without his sister acting foolish.

Tears sprang to her eyes at the thought. *If he should die, I want to die too, Great Spirit.* She thought of the eagle who had brought them here. Where was he now? In a nice quiet shelter of a tree, she thought angrily. No bird would try flying against this wind. He was lucky. He could find shelter easily. It was not so easy for humans.

Suddenly, she heard the cry of a coyote. It sounded very close by. "Little Brother, I'm going to have a quick look around." She didn't want a hungry coyote to find them—or their deer meat.

"All right, Sister." His voice was small, coming from inside the snow cave.

Autumn wriggled out of the cave door. As she stood up, the wind battered her and a blanket of white snow hit her in the face. It was no use—she could see nothing. She could barely open her eyes, and when she did, they were pierced by the unforgiving snow. The world had turned into a mass of swirling white demons. The wind, roaring like a giant through the tops of the pine trees, sent needles of ice to slap her in the face.

"Go away, you foolish coyote!" she yelled as loudly as she could. The howling stopped. She turned back to her brother.

In another moment, she had wedged herself back into the door of their snow cave, blocking the wind. Shivering, she pulled her deer skin as tightly around her as she could and hoped the falling snow would cover her up quickly enough to warm her.

The coyote howled again, but this time his voice came from farther away.

"Coyote Boy, are you warm enough?"

"Yes, are you?" His voice was almost a whisper amidst the roaring of the storm.

"I am warm enough," she answered, even though her hands and feet were beginning to feel numb. She wondered if that were good or bad.

"If you're so warm, Autumn, why are you shivering and I am not?" he asked.

Why did he have to notice that? "Must you argue continually?" She was too exhausted for this.

"Yes, because you do not always tell me everything. You try to keep secrets, Autumn."

It was true of course, and she no longer had the strength to argue. "Yes, sometimes I do keep secrets, but that is for your own good. Now you must trust me. I will be all right once the snow covers me. You must lie still now and try to think of pleasant things. I am through with talk."

"Will you tell me a story, Autumn?" Coyote Boy's voice sounded as if it were coming from far away. Had she dozed off?

"A story?" She was so tired.

"Yes, please."

Perhaps it was a good idea. Telling a story would keep her alert.

"All right, then, a story. I will tell the story of how Fisher went to the skyland and brought summer to the earth."

"Oh, I love that one."

"In the long-ago time," Autumn Dawn began, "when the animals could talk, Fisher went out to hunt. It was not easy . . ." Autumn stopped. Her teeth were chattering and it was hard to talk. *Telling a story will keep me warm. Especially a story about summer.*

I must stay awake.

"Autumn?" Coyote Boy stirred.

"It was not easy to hunt in those days because there was snow on the ground all the time. For it was always winter and never spring."

I must stay awake.

"The earth was frozen with winter's unrelenting chill," she continued. "The wind screamed through the trees like a lost spirit, searching in vain for its resting place." Like today, Autumn thought.

"Fisher could hardly see through the blowing snow and was about to give up his hunt when he saw a squirrel struggling to run through the deep snow. He pounced on the squirrel. 'Wait, do not kill me, Fisher, for I can tell you something important,' said the squirrel."

She struggled to keep talking, to tell the story of the fisher who brought summer to the earth, but soon Coyote Boy grew still.

Her instincts told her not to sleep, but she was too tired to fight it any longer. Her eyelids, heavy with fatigue, closed.

Chapter Thirteen

Autumn Dawn dreamed. Somewhere, far in the distance, through a swirl of white snow, someone was approaching her. The shape on the snowbound horizon was foggy, though, and she could not even tell if it was animal or human. She, however, felt no fear.

Autumn moved forward, toward the swirling white, toward the unknown being. Even though she was surrounded by snow, she felt no cold, for this was a different kind of place: a place not of the earth.

Slowly, as Autumn walked down the path of white, the brightness intensified. Now she could see the being clearer, and it was not human. Still, she was unafraid. The being shifted into focus. It was Eagle.

"Why are you here?" Eagle asked.

"I do not know. . . ." Autumn replied, confused.

"You must leave this place. It is not your time to be here."

"Leave?" To go back to what? That cold, unfriendly world she had left behind? "I do not wish to return."

"Where is your brother?" Eagle asked.

For a moment, Autumn was stunned. She had forgotten all about him.

"I . . . I don't know. . . ." she stammered.

Eagle glared at her, unspeaking.

"I suppose he is still there—where I left him, under the pine tree."

"Where you left him?" Eagle bellowed.

Autumn shrunk back in fear. "But I did not leave on purpose. I . . . I do not know how I got here. It is not my fault I am here."

"Nevertheless, you must fight your way back."

Fight her way back? She had no desire to go. "Please, let me stay. Bring my brother here also. You are powerful; you can bring him here."

"It is not his time yet, as it is not yours. You must be strong, Autumn Dawn Shines on Leaf. Much lies ahead for you."

Strong? Isn't that what she had been for these many months? She was tired of being strong. She just wanted to sleep forever in a place that was warm. A place like this. "Can I not stay here just a little while longer?"

"No, you must leave here at once. Go, now, to your brother."

Autumn Dawn knew she must do as Eagle said, but it was so hard. Would their journey never end? With regret, she turned away from Eagle.

But when she tried to walk back along the path of white, she could not move. Her legs would not work. She no longer even felt her feet beneath her.

What was wrong?

She turned back quickly to Eagle, but he was no

longer there. Instead, his voice called to her, "You must fight, Autumn Dawn. Fight your way back."

She turned to leave once again, but it was almost impossible. *Place one foot in front of the other, move a tiny distance.* It was warm here, so warm . . . she did not wish to go.

"Your brother needs you," the voice said.

She struggled against the overwhelming desire to sleep. To stay asleep forever.

"Autumn, please wake up," another voice, close by, cried.

"Coyote Boy?" She struggled to open her eyes. But her eyelids were heavy and they would not open.

Suddenly, something hit her face with a hard slap. Her eyes opened, but could not quite focus. Through the haze, she saw a young man. He leaned over her, his long loose hair falling forward. Could it be?

"White Otter?" she asked, uncertain. Perhaps she was in the spirit world with her friend.

But the young man said nothing. Then she heard another voice.

"I'm here, Autumn," Coyote Boy said as he took her hand. She hadn't seen him at first, even though he was kneeling next to White Otter all the time. Were they all finally together and happy once again?

Then, she looked closer at the young man and her eyes cleared. No, it was not White Otter, she thought with a heavy heart.

She was sure, though, that the little boy next to the man was her brother. She was not in the spirit world after all.

Autumn Dawn tried to pull Coyote Boy to her, but her body seemed stiff, unable to work.

"We must get her back to camp quickly," she heard the young man say to Coyote Boy.

Autumn lifted her head to look around. Through her haze she could see that she and Coyote Boy were in front of what looked like a snow cave. *Who had built it?* she wondered. She felt as if she should know, but she could not think. She laid her head back down.

Then she remembered, and her heart began to race. She had to protect Coyote Boy. But from what? She couldn't remember.

"Coyote Boy, are you all right?" With stiff arms, she reached out for him.

"Yes, Little Wolf is a friend. He is going to help us."

Little Wolf? *Who is Little Wolf?* But before she could speak again, she felt herself being lifted off the ground.

"Camp is not far," someone said, "Do you think you can walk?"

Walk? Walk where? Autumn wondered.

"Yes," a small voice answered. "I will be all right. I can help pull the sledge." It was her brother's voice.

"No, I will pull it. You take your walking stick and look out for enemies," the young man replied.

Look out for enemies. The words of the stranger sounded familiar to Autumn. Had she said them to Coyote Boy once, or had that been a dream?

As she felt herself being pulled through the snow, Autumn Dawn tried to make sense of what was happening to her, but the harder she tried, the more confused she became. She remembered a dream . . . or had it been . . . of a great blizzard? Coyote Boy was injured, and she had to save him. And there was an eagle. . . .

"Little Wolf!" she heard another voice now, a stranger's voice calling, shouting. "The hunting party— we were attacked."

"What?"

"Bwaan warriors. Father and Uncle were killed. Only I was able to escape. It was . . ." the voice trailed off.

There was silence for a moment. Then Autumn heard the young man's voice, hard and angry. "The Bwaan will pay for this outrage—later. Now we must hurry back to camp. These two are injured."

Someone was killed by the Bwaan. Even in her fog, Autumn knew the Bwaan were her enemy. Once again, fear gripped her heart. "Coyote Boy," she cried out.

"I am right here, Autumn," he answered.

"Do not concern yourself. Your brother is safe." The young man's voice was ragged, as if he were holding back a great sadness.

The rocking rhythm of the moving sledge continued through the snow, and soon put her to sleep.

When Autumn Dawn awoke, it was to the familiar warmth of a wigwam. A low fire burned in the center of the floor. With sleep-filled eyes, she looked around the lodge. *Where were Mother and Father?*

Then, the memories came flooding back. Her home was gone, her parents dead. A familiar pain gripped her heart.

She forced it away with questions. Whose lodge was this? And where was Coyote Boy? Autumn sat up and threw off the many bearskins she was covered with. She tried to stand, but pain lanced through her feet.

She looked down at them. Someone had removed her moccasins and foot coverings.

Her feet didn't look too bad. Not black, like some she had seen after being frozen, but they hurt unbearably. She sat down and began rubbing them. Just then someone entered the wigwam.

"They will hurt for a while, but you are lucky." It was a woman. She looked about the same age as Autumn's mother.

In deference to an elder, Autumn looked down, studying her feet as she continued to rub them.

"Where am I?" she asked softly. "And . . . where is my brother?"

"He is with my son. I will send him in shortly." The

woman sounded tired.

"*Miigwech.* Thank you for helping me," Autumn said.

"I am thankful that I could be of help to someone today," the woman said abruptly and quickly left.

It wasn't until the flap of the wigwam dropped that Autumn realized the woman had spoken her language. The woman was Anishinaabe! These were her people!

Suddenly Autumn wanted to know more. She had so many questions.

Then, she heard voices, distressed voices. Outside on the other side of camp perhaps? As she leaned toward the entrance to the wigwam and listened closer, she could make out the sounds of a woman wailing, as if in mourning. Yes, it was definitely someone grieving, but who had died?

Autumn's stomach turned over. What if she had found her people—only to watch them die of the white man's disease? She couldn't stand that again. She would find Coyote Boy and leave at once.

Autumn tried to stand up, but the pain in her feet shot through her whole body. Never mind, she must go. With difficulty she reached the door of the wigwam, pulled the bearskin aside and looked out.

Outside, she saw two women—the one she'd just met and a younger girl, not much older than she was. They were standing outside the only other wigwam in sight. Someone had died, and the women were in mourning.

Autumn Dawn looked quickly around the camp. There was no one else. Where was Coyote Boy? She turned and moved back into the wigwam.

My moccasins must be here somewhere. I must find my brother.

In a moment she spotted her moccasins, placed neatly in the corner of the wigwam. Autumn walked over to them, sat down, and rubbed her feet some more.

"Oh—you are awake."

Autumn looked up, startled. In the doorway stood a young man. For a moment she thought it was White Otter, but she knew better. Coyote Boy was behind him, but quickly darted past the man to her.

"You should not walk for a while," the young man said.

Autumn Dawn glanced at him, as Coyote Boy fell into her arms. He clung to her, holding on tightly.

"What is the matter, Little One?" she asked him.

"I was afraid you were going to die, Autumn. You looked frozen."

Autumn pulled away from him. "Look at my feet, Little Brother." She wiggled her toes painfully. "See, they still work, and they have not turned black. I will not lose them."

Coyote Boy continued to hold her tight. The young man still stood in the doorway. She studied him now more closely for the first time, and noticed that he was rather pleasant to look at.

"Your little brother is too curious. He left the wigwam when he heard us bring the slain ones back." While his face was friendly, the young man's voice held an angry edge to it. He was very upset.

"Is it the white man's disease? Is someone ill?" she asked, hoping that it was not true.

He said nothing for a moment, then he spoke. "My father and uncle were killed by Bwaan." He spat the last word out. "Your brother saw the bodies. My cousin and I retrieved them from the place where they fell."

A hunting party. Bwaan! She'd had a dream about someone calling out the name Little Wolf, talking about an attack.

She pulled Coyote Boy even closer and looked down. "I am sorry, but I do not remember how I came to be here."

The young man looked at her as if he just now saw her. He spoke slowly, carefully.

"You . . . when we set out this morning, our hunting party found you sitting up in a snowdrift, sleeping and nearly covered with snow, and your brother behind you inside in a snow cave. My elders told me to take you back to camp, while they went on to hunt. It looked like a fine day and after all the snowfall, animal tracks were plentiful.

"Your brother helped me wake you up," he added.

She couldn't remember. It all seemed like a dream.

"You almost froze to death," he said.

Autumn was flooded with mixed feelings. She was glad there was no disease here, but . . . suddenly she realized something.

"You were supposed to be with them, weren't you? You said your elders told you to take me back to camp. You saved me and my brother. . . . I am sorry."

Autumn looked down in shame. She was alive, but this young man's father and uncle were dead.

Maybe, if he had been with them, he could have helped save them. Surely he must hate her.

The young man moved into the wigwam. She knew he was standing right next to her, but she would not look at him.

He stood there for a moment, saying nothing. Then, he stooped down next to her.

His shoulder touched her own and Autumn quickly moved away. He did the same. Under normal circumstances, he would not be allowed to be alone with her like this. It was not considered proper. But now, the elders were distracted with their sorrow.

"I may have saved you, but you saved my life as well." He paused a moment, then went on.

"Your brother told me how far you have journeyed. You must be strong and clever to have survived such a long journey in winter."

Autumn kept her eyes down, holding Coyote Boy close. She was now far too embarrassed to look at the young man.

"If we had not found you," he continued, "and if I had gone on with the rest of the hunters . . . I, too, might be dead now. Then, who would care for my grandfather and the women?"

"I am sorry for the death of your loved ones," Autumn Dawn murmured, still looking down.

"In the spring, I will form a war party," he said. "We will push the Bwaan west of the Great River."

Autumn slowly looked up at him. His face was so close she felt overwhelmingly shy. She didn't know what to say.

"Grandfather says," he continued, "that the Great Spirit has a plan. That perhaps there was a reason I found you half frozen."

He was looking at her so intently that she lowered her eyes again. "But maybe," she said softly, "if you had not found me, you could have saved your loved ones."

"You make me sound too important. Our hunting party would have been outnumbered with or without me."

So, he was not a boastful young man. Autumn appreciated that quality. White Otter had not been boastful either.

Thoughts of White Otter flooded her with memories of a different life. It seemed so long ago. She felt her eyes fill with tears.

"I must go now," he said in embarrassment. "Mother just wanted me to bring your brother back to you." But he made no move to leave.

Autumn Dawn looked up at him. He must have noticed her tears because he looked away, respecting her privacy. She wanted him to both stay and leave at the same time.

"*Miigwech*. Thank you, again, for saving us. I just wish . . ." She felt her voice crack, and her throat closed up.

"Do not wish for things that cannot be," he said as he stood up, reluctantly.

He seemed so wise, and yet he looked little older than herself. He walked to the wigwam door.

"Wait," Autumn called out, feeling bold. "I am called Autumn Dawn Shines on Leaf." Names were usually not exchanged between people who had just met. Would he tell her his?

"I am Little Wolf," he said as he turned, and his gaze met hers.

Little Wolf, of course, the voice in her dream. His eyes were so warm and friendly that Autumn, looking into them, no longer felt quite so shy. "It is a fine name," she said.

He turned away and slipped out the bearskin door. Autumn sat still for a moment, conflicting emotions washing over her. She still felt like crying, but she was not sure if it was from sadness or joy.

Coyote Boy got off her lap and went to the door. "I like him," he said as he looked out at camp.

"Yes, I like him too." She stood up on her sore feet. She joined her brother at the door and watched Little Wolf walk away.

Looking up into the bright blue of the sky, Autumn Dawn suddenly felt hollow. It was as if the empty sky matched the emptiness in her heart. She thought of Mother, Father, and White Otter—all gone now.

But then, for just a brief moment, she thought she saw their faces in the sky. They were smiling down on her, telling her it was time to start a new life.

In another moment their faces faded. She felt dizzy, and had to look down until her eyes cleared.

She looked up again, searching the sky. But the faces were gone . . . replaced by a familiar figure.

It was Eagle, circling the small camp. *Did you bring me here*, she spoke silently, *to save Little Wolf? And if so, to what purpose?*

"Autumn, is this our new home?" Coyote Boy asked.

As if to answer, the magnificent bird flew through a streak of sunlight that bathed the eagle in a golden glow.

Tears of joy stung her eyes. Whatever else Eagle had in store for them, Autumn Dawn knew the answer to her brother's question.

"Yes, Little Brother. We are finally home."

AUTHOR'S NOTE

Although Autumn Dawn and her little brother Coyote Boy are fictional characters, their story is based on very real events that occurred in the late 1700s among the Lake Superior Anishinaabe.

The Anishinaabe, a large tribe of North American Indians, are commonly known as Ojibwe (which is sometimes spelled Ojibway or Ojibwa), or historic treaties, Chippewa. But *Anishinaabe* is what the people call themselves in their own language.

When European explorers first arrived in the Americas, they were looking for a route to the spices of the fabled Far East. When they realized they had not landed in China or the East Indies, they began to look around for gold and silver instead. But the real riches they found were not precious metals but new plants like potatoes, squash, and corn.

In the north, they also found a wonderful land of lakes and forests, full of wild animals like beaver, ermine, and fox. Eager to buy many furs to ship home to make fashionable clothes and hats, the Europeans traveled deep into the "wilderness" to visit native villages where they could trade for the precious pelts.

Some Europeans set up trading companies that sent in men to live and barter with the Indians, who were skilled hunters and trappers. Other companies built posts where the Indians themselves could bring in furs to trade. In return, native families could get useful goods—iron pots, knives and axes, metal needles, bolts of cloth, and colored glass beads.

But while the Europeans brought some things the native peoples were interested in, they also brought something undesirable: deadly germs.

The American Indians had never been exposed to the foreigners' germs before; their bodies did not have any built-up immunity to diseases common in Europe. When Indian hunters returned to their villages after visiting the trading posts, they often brought back germs in their bodies—and on blankets and other items they had received in trade or as gifts.

The results were terrible. Many men, women, and children died of sicknesses as common as influenza, what we today call the flu. But of all the illnesses, the most deadly that raced through the native communities was smallpox.

While researching the culture of the Anishinaabe people in the Lake Superior region, I came across a story that an old Ojibwe woman once told to Frances Densmore, an anthropologist who collected stories and studied native ways in the early 1900s.

This elderly Ojibwe lady told Densmore of a young woman she'd heard about who had survived a smallpox epidemic that had devastated her village. Everyone else in the village had died or had already left camp when this teenage girl was forced to flee the illness, alone. On foot, and through an entire winter, the girl traveled by herself through the woods, surviving by her wits, until finally finding another Ojibwe village. Here she was accepted and found a new home.

I gave this real girl a fictional life, including a little brother to take care of. In my story, they begin their courageous journey in 1781. This was the year when a very bad smallpox epidemic struck the native families of the Lake Superior region.

I imagined Autumn Dawn and Coyote Boy living in northern Wisconsin, not far from where the community of Lac Du Flambeau is today. In my story, they travel north and west to the area near Ashland where today's Bad River band of the Ojibwe is located. However, this story could have happened anywhere in the Lake Superior region, during this or another deadly outbreak of smallpox.

Sadly, much oral history was lost with those who died, as tribal elders—the keepers of the stories—were especially hard hit by the illness. But as a people, the Anishinaabe did survive. Into the 21st century, they have preserved a rich culture and a deep knowledge of the northern woodlands.

The Anishinaabe did not always live in this region. They had once lived on the east coast of North America, near the Atlantic. Over 500 years, they slowly moved westward, up the St. Lawrence River. Eventually, they settled in the Lake Superior area, in what today is Ontario (in Canada), and in Michigan, Wisconsin, and Minnesota.

Like the Anishinaabe, other tribes were also moving slowly to the west, partly to move away from the Europeans—who were settling the east in greater numbers. More and more soldiers, missionaries, and settlers were building forts, churches, farms, and towns. In a chain reaction, each native group was pushed westward, crowding into the territory of their neighbors.

In the Lake Superior area in the 1700s, there was much conflict between the Anishinaabe and the native tribes just to the west, the *Dakota*, who were known to the Anishinaabe as *Bwaan* (and to the whites as the "Eastern Sioux").

During this time, the fur trade was dominated by French traders. To make the Anishinaabe their friends, the French gave them help, and often guns. This helped the Anishinaabe to push the Dakota people westward across the Mississippi and St. Croix rivers into Minnesota.

In the late 1700s, after several wars, the British and then the new U.S. government took over the trade in the Lake Superior area. But soon, the Americans turned to logging, mining, and farming. They increased pressure on native tribes, causing them either to move west or go to war to defend their territory. One by one, Indian nations were driven from their homes or forced to live on small reservations.

Today, though, native nations like the Anishinaabe/Ojibwe are strong in spirit and growing in numbers. Some Anishinaabe families live on reservation lands around Lake Superior. Others live in large cities such as Minneapolis and elsewhere throughout the U.S. and Canada.

To find out more about the Ojibwe, you may wish to read some of the books listed at the end of this book. But the best way to learn more is to meet community members of the Anishinaabe in person. You can visit tribal museums or visit pow-wows that are open to the public. Pow-wows are public gatherings where tribal members gather to dance, make music, share food, socialize, and honor their elders.

At these festive pow-wows or at other public events, native peoples welcome those who are interested in learning more about their ways—and who are willing to take the time to be good listeners.

GLOSSARY

Here are some special words used in the book. Ojibwe words are in italics.

awl—a tool made from a sharp bone. It is used to punch holes in softened hides, so sinew can be "threaded" through. This is Autumn's "needle" that she uses to make their clothes, moccasins, and hand-coverings.

Big Water, *gichigami*—Lake Superior

bwaan—Ojibwe name for the Eastern Sioux, or Dakota, people.

gichi-manidoo—great spirit

Great River, *gichi-ziibi*—Mississippi River

maiingan—wolf

makak—a birchbark container. These had many uses, the most common being storage. Before the traders came with kettles, people cooked in a makak in this way: they heated small rocks in a fire, then dropped the hot rocks into the water in the watertight birchbark "pot." Eventually, the water became hot enough to cook the food.

medicine bag—many American Indians would carry a small bag, made out of animal skin. In it they would keep the essentials—herbs for healing, tobacco, maybe a little rice or sweetgrass.

miigwech—thank you

migizi—bald eagle

nibi—water; the "sacred source" or "life-giver."

moccasin, *makizin*—a type of comfortable soft shoe, made from animal skin, offering protection for the foot.

poultice—a messy mash made up of healing plants (usually roots) held together by a piece of cloth or animal skin. It was placed on a wound and kept there for a time.

shakers—musical rhythm instruments; these were often used during dances and ceremonies.

sinew—the tendons of an animal; in this case, of a deer. Using it like thread, Autumn could sew her and Coyote Boy's moccasins and hand-coverings together.

sledge—another name for a sled.

snares—hand-made traps for animal, often fashioned from strong twine made from a basswood tree. Or, a typical rabbit snare was a net made out of nettle fiber. There are many different kinds of snares. They work by tangling a small animal in their net or in a noose that tightens to keep the animal from escaping.

Another kind of snare lures an animal with bait, then lifts the trapped animal high up in the air, to keep it from being eaten by a larger animal before the hunter who set the trap comes back to check it.

snow snake—a children's game. First, something (a sled or even a small boy) is dragged through the snow to make a firm track. Then, narrow "snakes" would be made out of wood. Each child would get a turn to give their wooden snake a sliding push down the track. Whoever's snake went the farthest was the winner.

spikenard—a bush with large leaves, small greenish white flowers, and red or purple berries. Indians used the root mashed up into a poultice (a soft, moist mash) on wounds to decrease swelling. Related to ginseng.

tanning—to "tan" a hide, first the flesh was scraped off with a sharpened rock. Then the hide was soaked overnight, or even for a day or two. For extra softness, deer brains are rubbed on the scraped hide (there is a substance in them that softens the hide so it becomes much easier to work with). To finish the process, a fire is made in a hole in the ground and the hide is hung over it. The smoldering fire gives the hide a golden color.

trader's steel—before the traders arrived, fires could be started in several ways. One was to strike two very hard stones together to make a spark. The trick was to get the spark to light some "punk" or tinder—some easy-to-light material held in the same hand as one of the stones.

Another method used a little bow to spin a stick very rapidly. The stick was pressed down hard on a piece of cedar, with a little pile of shredded bark ready to catch fire when the stick and cedar got hot enough from the friction.

Later, traders brought steel. Then, a piece of flint (a hard stone) could be struck against a piece of "trader's steel," a more reliable way to start a fire. Autumn Dawn would have been familiar with this method but did not have any trader's steel with her because she left her home camp in such a hurry.

Wenabozho—a mythic folk hero of the Anishinaabe people. He was both teacher and magician. Sometimes he played tricks on people to teach a lesson. He could turn himself into any animal, plant, or even a rock, if need be. His grandmother was Nokomis. Wenabozho is spelled differently in different places. *Win-na-boo-zhoo, Nanabush, Manabozho,* and *Nanabosho* are just some of the different spellings I have found. An Anglo-American writer named Henry Wadsworth Longfellow mistakenly called him *Hiawatha* in a famous poem.

wigwam, *waaginogaan*—the traditional winter home of the Anishinaabe. This house was built by covering a latticework of bent saplings with cattail mats to make the walls, with a layer of birchbark to cover the roof and protect the outside. It had a dirt floor, and a hole was left in the roof to let out the smoke from the indoor fire. In the winter, a fire was almost always kept burning inside the wigwam.

wiindigoo—a giant, sometimes evil.

Wild Rice Moon—the name given to September. September is the usual time for gathering wild-rice. That is when this story begins.

wild ginger—a low-growing plant found on the forest floor; it has heart-shaped leaves of dark green. The root is used mashed up, as a poultice, on fractures.

Note: For the Anishinaabe words, I have chosen to use the double-vowel style of spelling, based on *A Concise Dictionary of Minnesota Ojibwe,* by John D. Nichols and Earl Nyholm (University of Minnesota Press).

In other books, you may see words spelled with a single-vowel (i.e., *Anishinabe* instead of *Anishinaabe*). But the doubled-vowel is preferred today by educators who wish to encourage a uniform spelling of the Ojibwe language.

RESOURCES

The Adventures of Nanabush: Ojibway Indian Stories, by Emerson and David Coatsworth, illustrated by Frances Kagige (Margaret K. McElderry Books/ Atheneum, 1980). Told by Sam Snake and others. Full-color paintings by an Ojibway artist depict traditional tales. (Contains "The Helpful Turtle" story that Autumn Dawn tells Coyote Boy.)

The Birchbark House, by Louise Erdrich (Hyperion, 1999). A beautiful novel, for ages 9-12, of four seasons in 1847 as seen through the eyes of a 7-year-old girl, *Omakayas*, or Little Frog, on Lake Superior's Madeline Island, including a winter when an outbreak of smallpox hits the island.

Giving: Ojibwa Stories and Legends from the Children of Curve Lake, edited by Georgia Elston, illustrated by the children of Curve Lake Reserve (Waapoone Publishing, 1985, Lakefield, Ontario). Ojibwa children from Canada wrote and illustrated these traditional and original stories.

The Good Path: Ojibwe Learning and Activity Book for Kids, by Thomas Peacock, photographs by Marlene Wisuri (Afton Historical Society Press, 2002, Afton, Minnesota). Presents traditional tales and a history of the Ojibwe, with discussion of timeless values.

The Mishomis Book: The Voice of the Ojibway, by Edward Benton-Banai, illustrated by Joe Liles (Red School House, 1988, St. Paul, Minnesota). A cultural and historical account of the Anishinaabe. Benton-Banai is a Wisconsin Ojibway of the Fish Clan and a Spiritual Teacher of the Lac Court Orielles Band.

The Ojibwe, by Raymond Bial (Benchmark Books, 2000). Modern and historical photographs of people engaged in everyday tasks; includes a section listing many useful resources, including print materials, websites, and information on tribal organizations.

Nanabosho, Soaring Eagle, and the Great Sturgeon, by Joe McLellan, illustrated by Rhian Brynjolson (Pemmican Publishers, 1993, Winnipeg). A picture book with a story within a story. A grandfather in modern times tells his two granddaughters a traditional tale that teaches a lesson about conserving natural resources.

Native American Stories, by Joseph Bruchac, illustrated by John Kahionhes Fadden (Fulcrum Publishing, 1991, Golden, Colorado). This book contains stories from several different native traditions, including Anishinaabe. (Includes "How Fisher Went to the Skyland.")

Native People of Wisconsin, by Patty Loew (Wisconsin Historical Society Press, 2003, Madison). Introduces students to the tribal traditions, history, and life today of the Indian nations that live in Wisconsin, including the Ojibwe. Loew is a member of the Bad River Band of Lake Superior Ojibwe.

The Sacred Harvest: Ojibway Wild Rice Gathering, by Gordon Regguinti, photographs by Dale Kakkak (Lerner Publications, 1992, Minneapolis). An 11-year-old Ojibway boy learns how to become a wild ricer with the help of his grandfather. Takes place in modern-day Minnesota.

Shannon, An Ojibway Dancer, by Sandra King, photographs by Catherine Whipple (Lerner Publications, 2001, Minneapolis). Shannon is a modern 13-year-old Ojibway girl who lives in Minneapolis and dances as a fancy shawl dancer at powwows across Minnesota. Many photographs.

Tales the Elders Told, by Basil Johnson, illustrated by Shirley Cheechoo (Royal Ontario Museum, 1981, Toronto). Nine tales translated into English from the Ojibway. (Includes "How Dogs Came to Be," the story of the fishermen and the two giants that Autumn sings to Coyote Boy.)

A NOTE FOR EDUCATORS

We are honored that *Time of the Eagle* has been reviewed by the 20-member Intertribal Editorial Board of the Council for Indian Education (Dr. Hap Gilliland, president) and has received its recommendation as being good material for use in schools. This board of native educators is a national program that examines materials before they are published to ensure that a book positively portrays Native American values and ideals, as well as the culture of the particular tribe about which it is written.

Stephanie Golightly Lowden lives in Madison, Wisconsin. She is not of Indian heritage; Golighty is a traditional Scottish name that reflects her father's roots. For this book, with the help of kind advice from Ojibwe acquaintances around the region, she and the publisher have tried to seek a balance between actual history and the fictional magic that creates a freshly told story.

All stories are beginnings. They are small sparks that encourage us to take the next step forward in action and exploration.

For free downloadable teacher materials and other resources on native history and culture today in the Upper Midwest, we invite you to visit our website.

Blue Horse Books
www.bluehorsebooks.org